OZ

ONE OF TEN

JACK REYNOLDS

PUBLISHED BY FIDELI PUBLISHING

~ Even though the book Oz, One of Ten is fictional all of the story lines are based upon true occurrences.

It was written to open the eyes of parents while wishing to permanently close the eyes of pedophiles. ~

PREFACE

The author's comment

Good men are not distinguished by the fact that they have never disciplined their children, whether it is with a threat of using a belt or a spanking born of affection due to concern for a child's safety or wellbeing. In the father scenario; good men stand out solely because of their compassion for being proud and protective. It is a God like feeling that resonates and settles in the hearts of men that look beyond their own self-satisfaction. But … to those who ponder the thought of yielding to temptation and violating a child; we use a paraphrase of biblical proportion:

> *"It would be better for you to cut it off*
> *than to use it to destroy the lives of your or our children.*
> *There shall be neither forgiveness nor mercy"*

Secrets

When it comes to preventive ways to counter the act of pedophilia, I have a list as long as a good mother, but one comes to mind that has more resolve than any other. I've attended book signings with conversations that tend to bring out tearful emotions from women because they relate to the story line as something that has occurred in their own childhood. They breakdown emotionally and reflect that they have never told anyone but, "It happen to me."

Well, without further ado; statistics show that a pedophile has as many as ninety (90) children that he has sexually abused during his lifetime. That woman in tears may have been his first. By not exposing her predator, she has contributed to the raping and ruining of the lives of children to come.

Because of this, we say that **secrets** have no place in the world of children are threatened by pedophilia. We must teach our children that there are no **secrets.** We must speak to children in terms that take away the number-one cloak of a child predator.

Also, women who have been sexually abused, no matter when, should speak up and take down an on-going threat to children everywhere. They must realize that the man did not stop after violating them; he has gone on and on, perhaps with with someone you know or one of yoru relatives. Perhaps he will never be caught at his game of **secrets.** As he ages, he only gets more cunning at what he does to so many. There is no end until he is dead and has left his **secrets** behind with his many victims.

I have read that a true pedophile has convinces himself that he hasn't done anything wrong. We must assure him that he has.

†

"The act of child abuse constitutes a disturbing danger and a colossal impact on society. Children deserve our love and protection which requires constant vigilance though vigilance alone is not enough. We need also responsibility coupled with commitment to honestly address pedophilia regardless to who is involved. This is not a selected or random cause; but one which impacts the very existence of humanity if left unchecked"

— Dr. Condie M. Clayton
Educator and retired police officer

†

†

CHAPTER ONE

3:15 a.m.

Oz jerked his head up and away from the comfort of his pillow. The bedroom appeared pitch-black; for a split second he wasn't sure where he was. He wasn't sure who he was. He wasn't sure what he was or what was real; was it the lights out in the darkness, or the darkness that surrounded him inside?

For hundreds of years as an angel he had awakened to the bright explosion of heavenly light, light brighter than the morning sun, so bright that everything around him appeared to be white. Even the shadows of moving subjects were as bright as freshly fallen snow.

Tonight, in his peripheral vision, the twinkling of city lights off in the distance caught his attention. He sat upright on the side of a bed looking out into the night. Up to this point sounds were not a factor.

Suddenly he felt and heard a quick rush of air being inhaled into his nostrils and down deep into his chest as if he were coming alive and breathing for the first time. After a pause he exhaled, seemingly loud enough to question if the roaring sound had come from within or from something or someone else. He turned his attention back into the darkness of the room and waited for his eyes to adjust well enough to evaluate his surroundings.

"Jason," a voice startled him. It was warm and filled with concern yet unrecognizable "are you all right?" He struggled within himself to identify the female that had broken the silence.

"Baby, what's wrong?" Without answering either question he turned and sought the origin of the voice. She touched him; he quickly pulled away as if he had no knowledge of what it was like to be touched by a woman.

"What's wrong Jason?" He still did not answer. He placed his hand against his chest and recognized that he was naked. He touched his own thigh and down onto one knee and without hesitating back up his body. In a continuous motion he cupped his hands over his face and again drew in a strong burst of air.

"Baby, are you okay?" Still, there was no answer from him. He felt the bed rustle as the female apparently sat up and moved against him.

"You must have had a nightmare." He remained puzzled and continued to gaze around in the darkness. He sniffed the air after smelling an unfamiliar fragrance. As the female placed her head on his shoulder he recognized that the sweet smell was coming from the woman that was continuously asking questions.

He was thinking of what he might say. He had questions of his own, questions like; who in the hell is Jason? Why is it so dark and why does she smell of flowers? His eyes finally adjusted to the darkness enough that he could see the sparkle in the whites of her eyes. She spoke again.

"Baby your scaring me, please say something."

Who are you? He questioned expecting her to hear his thoughts. Again he asked without opening his mouth; who are you and where are we and why is it so dark here?

She pulled on his arm attempting to pull him back down onto the bed. He yielded and lay down beside her. She whispered,

"I love you. If anything ever happened to you I wouldn't want to live." He slightly squirmed, as he had never done before. Closing his eyes he flexed his muscles from chest to buttocks to thigh, he had yet to say a word out loud.

He refocused his attention out into the night, looking at the streetlights and car lights moving in the distance. Momentarily he thought he heard voices from the world outside. Once again, he inhaled as Helen curled up closer against him and squeezed him in an affectionate way.

This time the fragrance of her hair rushed even deeper into his chest. Turning his head toward her, he took in another deep breath. He realized that this was a first for him. He had never smelled anything like her.

He reached over to her with his left hand and touched her petite shoulder. She adjusted her body and moaned in a comforting way. Turning completely onto his side, he faced her and ran his hand along the curves of her body, feeling her breast and the passionate response his touch had caused.

She felt warm and exciting, differently from anything he could ever recall. Her skin was the color of chocolate and felt like silk to his fingertips. While pulling her tightly to his chest, he rocked her slightly with a comforting movement as she fell deeper asleep. In a few moments, he went back to sleep and back to his own heavenly world.

A few days later in the wee hours of a cold and snowy February morning, Jason lay in his king-sized bed next to Helen. Just like Oz, he was mysteriously awakened by a feeling that someone else was in the room besides he and Helen.

Finding himself a little uneasy in the dark and certainly a little apprehensive of his most recent string of nightmares, he looked over at Helen. She was fast asleep.

He decided to ask her the infamous and age-old question; the question that most people ask when they awaken in the middle of the night. 'Honey, are you asleep?' As usual, here and all over the world, there was no answer.

The vertical blinds at the sliding glass doors to the balcony were wide open, allowing him to look out into the night at his favorite view of the hills of East Pittsburgh. It was spectacular as usual. In the foreground was the challenging community of Homewood, followed by a view of most of the college community of Oakland. Further out into the night was a sparkling view of the skyline of downtown Pittsburgh.

He stood gazing with awe at the beauty of it all, and yet as he looked out into the night he wondered what might be going on in some of the homes and apartments between his view and the US Steel building in the middle of downtown. He was sure that most were safely fast asleep like Helen and his daughter. Others were about to wake and get ready for what ever their daily task might be.

He wondered how many were praying for something new or different or hoping that something had changed for the better during the night while they were sleeping. And then, for some strange reason, he wondered how much misery was being inflicted upon those that were vulnerable and subjected to conflict and abuse.

He wondered how much evil was lurking out there in the night just looking for someone's happiness to destroy. Longing to make someone else as miserable as they'd become. 'They,' are typically up to no good, especially in the middle of the night when idle and empty minds do their most destructive work.

He also thought about Sissy, who was laying he bed in the next room. She was their twelve-year-old adopted daughter who had gone through hell with her natural parents before coming to live with them. For more than nine years of her life she had suffered mental and sexual abuse beyond his imagination. He breathed a sigh of relief just knowing that at least both of these females were now safe and secure after all they had been through just a year and a half ago.

As he continued to meditate and gaze out the window, he was briefly startled. In the dark shadows of the room, out of the corner of his eye he thought he saw something move. Like an old newsreel, visions of children crying-out flashed before him, at first slowly, then faster and faster. They weren't laughing and playing as children usually do, these children were praying. They were reaching out to him for help.

He lay as still as he could in an attempt to not awaken the female again. The sheets absorbed his perspiration as his body responded to the pace of the children's pleas. Familiar faces, voices and small hands were reaching and pulling at his arms. Something inside him yielded enough for another to speak out from within him.

"Am I dreaming? A moment ago I was lying in the peacefulness of my bed dreaming I was something or someone else. Now, I'm caught in an accelerated review of some kind." He gently slid his body away from Helen and stood up, hoping it would all go away.

He placed his hands over his ears but it had no affect, the voices continued. The lights outside seemed to flash with the rhythm of the voices.

"Stop it!" All the lights stood still and the voices suddenly stopped at his command. "Am I going crazy? What's happening to me?" He glanced down at Helen as she lay curled in the sheets, unaware that he was losing his mind as she lay there sleeping.

"Mr. Oz, please help me. I don't know who else to turn to. You're the only one that seems to hear our voices. My name is Denise and I need to tell someone my story. I live in Homewood just outside of your window."

She sounds five or six years old. Why is this young child calling me Oz? My name is Jason and peacefully lying here beside me is my woman.

"Little girl I don't know how to help you. I can't see you and I don't know where you are." Jason squeezed the palms of his hands tighter against his ears. "My God, what's wrong with me?"

He lay back down next to Helen and wrapped his arms around her in an attempt to reestablish some level of reality. Helen did not awaken. Jason was alone, yet felt as if the room was crowded with children.

He closed his eyes and the crowded room clearly appeared before him. He quickly opened his eyes to the darkness of the room with the lights still sparkling outside his patio window. After looking around in the darkened room, he got up and stood naked at the glass patio door.

The skyline of downtown Pittsburgh flaunted its beauty in the distance. He didn't recall seeing the skyscrappers and the neon lights earlier. *Maybe this nightmare is over,* he thought.

He resisted looking back into the room behind him. He stood perfectly still and listened for the slightest sound, but he heard nothing. He wanted to turn around and look at Helen but his courage was eluded him.

He felt a small cold finger touch the back of his right leg. The curly hair stood up on the back of his neck as chills momentarily stunned him. He was mildly paralyzed by fear.

Slowly he turned his head and looked down over his right shoulder. He saw two small eyes staring up at him. Instantly he yanked his leg away and stumbled back against the wall near the headboard.

"I need to tell you my story, Mr. Oz."

"I am *not* Mr. Oz."

"I came home last week after spending the summer with my dad," she continued as if she hadn't heard him tell her he was not Oz.

"My momma's boyfriend was babysitting us while she worked the night shift; she's a nurse at the hospital. One night just after momma left, my sister and I were talking and he burst into our bedroom in a rage.

"'I'm sick of you two telling me about how great your daddy is,' he yelled. 'Now shut up and go to bed!' he said at the top of his voice."

"Why are you telling me this?" How did you get in here? Little girl, you've got to go home. I don't know how you got in here but I know you've got to go home."

"My sister and I hated him." Again she ignored Jason and continued her tale.

Here we go again, he thought. After a quick scared chill ran down his spine, he turned and looked around for a second or two. He decided there was nothing there and that it was time for him to get back into bed and cuddle up with his sleeping beauty.

Within a few minutes he got a second dose of chills. He had just finished squirming around trying to make himself as comfortable as possible when he felt the faint breeze of someone's breath blowing against his ear and upper neck.

"Please," he thought he heard some one say.

"Helen," he said, "there's someone in our room again." Helen was still deeply asleep and did not answer.

Again a breath feathered against him. He swatted at his own neck as if a bug had landed there. Something slightly bumped against his left foot causing him to freeze. After the hesitation, he snuggled closer to the body lying next to him.

Suddenly, he felt something blatantly grab his foot and was nearly pulled out of bed by his left ankle. This time he wasn't just startled, this time he was scared shitless. After quickly pulling his leg back up onto the bed, he regained his composure and again looked into the dark areas of the room.

His bedroom door remained closed, just as it had been. He knew no one could have come in without him knowing. He bravely moved to an upright position in his bed but didn't see or hear anything or anyone.

He paused for a moment still looking around the dark room for a possible intruder. He made up his mind to get up and turn on the lightswitch across the room. Before he planted his feet onto the floor, the room began to come alive with the help of his vivid imagination, the darkness was now blazing with superstitious possibilities.

In the corner behind the closed door he thought he had briefly seen something move. He focused his eyes and concentrated on a shadow that seemed to slightly move again.

Now he was getting uneasy. The more he focused, the more he could see. The children were back. At first threre were only two, then the vague shapes of more. They were sitting and standing along the far wall of his room about eight feet past the foot of his bed.

"Helen!" he said excitedly, "Helen wake up! I'm having a nightmare and I need you to wake up and talk to me. Helen! Wake up, I said. Wake up right now!"

"Okay, okay I'm awake. What do you want?"

"I'm having a very bad dream"

"Okay, honey, just go back to sleep, it'll go away," she said without ever opening her eyes or really waking up.

He couldn't go back to sleep … More was going on in his own room than he ever thought possible. After getting up a little courage, he shook it all off and convinced himself that it was just another badass dream.

He decided to get up and make his way to the bathroom where the lights were bright and the room would be clear of any shadows or images of children. He opened the bedroom door and rushed into the bathroom.

After a few minutes, he thought he faintly heard a baby crying. He listened closely as the sound faded away leaving him even more uneasy than he was when he came in. Just looking into the mirror caused him to visualize slight differences in his own appearance. *Enough is enough,* he thought as he hesitantly turned off the lights and heading back to his bed.

"What in the hell is going on here?"

Now there were many more children in the hall and in his bedroom along the wall. They were sitting and standing and seemed to be everywhere. The sight of so many was frightening enough but it got worse; they suddenly began to speak.

Voices of children, many children, began to call out in the night. Children, both male and female, seemed to be clawing at Jason's mind. He made it back into his bed but they didn't stop. They kept right on telling stories and begging for him to listen and help them.

He patiently began to listen, knowing that like any of his other dreams, these too would all go away in a few minutes. Instead, on and on it went. Occasionally one voice would be more distinct than the others, causing Jason to sit up and to pay more attention in an attempt to understand just what meaning, if any, these nightmares might have.

His attention was drawn to a young girl in the crowd, she was between the ages of six to eight years old. She seemed to have a strong vocabulary for such a young age, almost as if she had lived well beyond her years.

She was very well rehearsed about the story she needed to tell. Unlike the others, her bid for his attention was in the form of a warning instead of asking for help. Yet, just like the others, she indicated that she wanted to show him something that was going on or that had gone on some time before this day.

With both hands reaching out toward Jason in a give-me fashion, she pleaded. Once she got his attention she asked, "Do you hear the babies crying?"

He listen closer and quite distinctly heard the cry of infants.

"They are as young as four months and unable to pass on even the slightest thought of what they have gone through. I want you to come with me and get them. I want you to help them, Mr. Oz, but you must use extreme caution.

"I'll show you how they hurt us so badly. We don't want him to hurt you, too. I must make you aware of his sting. Please, please just come with me and try to take away the control and power the beast has over the helpless.

"You can stop him. He's the one that has poisoned many minds. This one is the mentor—"

Before she could continue he interrupted, "Little girl, what is your name?" Jason was becoming impatient and found himself speaking out in his own dream, "I can't go with you because you're not real. You're just some sort of dream that I can't explain, besides … I'm not Mr. Oz."

"My name is Victoria and I have been around for along time. Yes, I am real; I do exist," the small child insisted. "You can see and hear us because you've been chosen to avenge us. We are the judges and you are the avenger. You're the only one who can help these and many other children just like them."

Jason was confused by everything happening to him; mainly because these dreams all felt and sounded so real. He found himself again trying to reach Helen and wake her or ask Helen wake him, which would seem to be more realistic.

Suddenly he began to realize that one moment he recognized Helen, the next moment he had no idea of who she or why she was lying there beside him. For a brief second he wasn't even sure who *he* was. Was he Jason going crazy or was he this Oz person being overwhelmed by voices in the night?

As Jason, he was hoping the children would just go away or go home. As Oz, he felt compassion and the need to listen. As Oz, he knew why they had come to him.

Like the blinking lights at a distance out in the night, his mind took him from one person to another and from one state of mind to another, flashing sometimes slowly and at other times quickly. He went from Oz to Jason, from Jason to Oz, from disbelief to the knowing of the truth.

When he recognized his humble self as Jason he wanted Helen to wake him. When he felt the strength of Oz within him, he felt the anger of a god and wanted the children to lead him to his enemy.

For many nights Jason listen to these stories and continued to just write them off as terrible dreams to awaken from and to go on as if they had no real meaning. In recent months they had become more and more vivid to the point that one night he had risen and gone into the bathroom and in the mirror on the wall he caught a glimpse of someone else — someone that looked just like him but with glaring angry redish eyes. This person had visibly flexing muscles from his jawbone down to the horizon of his shoulders.

The glimpse he caught in the mirror was a warrior, not the kind and understanding man he had become. This warrior seemed to know something was very wrong somewhere nearby and also in many distant places. This was a warrior who felt an urge to destroy predators.

Jason again shook it off and attributed it to his ongoing problems with finding peaceful sleep.

As weeks went by, Jason's feeling of being intertwined with the being the children referred to as Oz became stronger. The pleas of the children traveled with Jason into the daytime and caused a sense of sadness.

There were nights when the woman that he lay next to and the room he was in began to fade into non-existence. During these times, it was the children who became truly real. More and more Jason was becoming Oz.

As Oz, he began to feel the pain of the children. Jason would stay quiet as the dialogue between the voices of the children and himself as Oz took over. He had truly begun to wonder if he was the sleeping angel named Oz. Where did that leave the humble and unknown man called Jason?

On this night Jason took in a deep breath and stood at the side of his bed, facing the children. He glanced down at them and to his own surprise he responded with a fearless and strong voice from within, "I'll help you." He'd never heard himself speak with this voice before.

"I'll help and protect you and I'll send those who have harmed you to hell! There will be no more suffering for your spirits."

The voices of the children had convinced Jason to listen and learn. Now they wanted him to submit to his urge to react and become Oz.

The stories continued to multiply. Each one became clear to Oz and more realistic to Jason. Remnants of Jason's soul whispered and continued with questions. *What can I do to for so many? How can I answer prayers that are meant for God Himself? Where do I start? Where do I go? How do I get there?* And the most puzzling question, *How could anyone remove these horrific things that have already occurred, out of their memories and away from their past?*

Oz's soul responded differently. His proud and unforgiving nature was telling him to just get there quickly and deal with each beast one at a time, just as it had dealt with these children. He would put it out of its misery. For every man that has found pleasure in the taking of innocence from a child or found delight in a child's cry for mercy, he could with Jason's help finally satisfy his need to strike back with a vengeance.

One after another the eyes of each child told their stories....

In Pittsburgh a two-year-old was taken out into a wooded area on freezing night and left to die by its father.

In Boston a four-year-old was thrown from a six-story apartment balcony after being mercilessly raped by a babysitting neighbor.

In Washington, D.C. an adoptive mother and father imprisoned their eight-year-old son in a basement closet to be tormented at their leisure for spiritual and sexual satisfaction according to their belief in self-cleansing.

In Seattle, a gay male took it upon himself to teach a five-year-old the true pleasure of same sex fondling, which led to a forceful violent penetration until the child yielded to his death.

A woman in an Atlanta day care center encouraged four young girls under the age of five to dance in the nude for her before teaching them to fondle each other. This ultimately led to her use of a dildo on each of them while they continued dancing to the musical beat. One of the children died. The woman was quoted as saying she just wanted to satisfy her desire to teach children at an early age that "naughty things were fun to do."

A prominent Alabama minister took a crackhead mother's ten-year-old as his wife in the name of the Lord Jesus Christ. Claiming, he took her from the grasp of the devil to teach her the ways of Christ.

In LA, New York, Chicago, Miami, Houston and big and small cities across the country and around the world, adult men and women were justifying their abuses in many deferent ways. They wanted what they were doing to be understood and accepted as being a benefit to their innocent victims. They even proclaimed that there was nothing wrong with consenting adult/child relationships.

Oz knew better and began to plan eye-opening events for those who were predators of innocent babies. He was going on a mission but he could not do it without cooperation from Jason's mind and body.

Jason and Oz were one being with two separate souls. Jason, handicapped by things such as mind-burdening morals, reasoning, and common sense, was being overtaken by Oz who was determined to satisfy his need to avenge on behalf of suffering children. Jason's constant infusion of rationality, humanity and cautions were no match for Oz's hunger to permanently punish those that have justified their evil acts with selfish delusions and pathetic excuses including horror stories of their own.

Oz intended no mercy. He was bent on sending every one of these offenders to God for judgment right now, while the rot was still strong in their hearts and long before their plans of asking for forgiveness could be implemented.

They were also beings with two separate minds, who often argued from within while in a state of subliminal spiritualism. Jason, as a man, could never recall the debates with his wayward angel counterpart, yet his reasoning often held at bay Oz's desire to punish the diseased bloodline of pedophiles.

Pedophiles seek the very young to satisfy their sexual needs and more times than not they regard an opportunity with a child as a gift from heaven or a temptation beyond their ability to resist. They take advantage of being bigger and stronger than their victims and they relish the chance to act as gods. They toy with their potential victim while outsmarting those who were normally cautious and apprehensive parents.

Their sexual satisfaction comes with rage and without forethought or mercy. Their passion is to fulfill their own desires to dominate with a god-like power over their child victims. They often reach the kind of sexual heights that could never be achieved in the presence of another adult; one that sets them, in their own minds, above ordinary people.

Oz, in his own realm, has the spirit of a bloodline of angels that can feel the despair and suffering of others. He cannot resist the desire to sacrifice himself to protect the helpless. Only heaven knows why or how the best of men are instilled with courage enough to step between a predator and what he or she chooses as prey.

Life doesn't seem to identify and punish this type of predator, but those like Oz do. Like a serpent, a pedophile lurks behind many cloaks and disguises. They go unrecognized in most cases even by the children who are being violated — even as they are violated.

They embed themselves into the lives of many with their deceptive acts of holiness and affection, only to drag the innocent minds into a world of broken spiritual self-esteem. It doesn't end there; their cunning and ruthless behavior with children is always justified by deceptive reasoning that often wins the hearts of those who wish to believe and forgive them. Statements and excuses are made, like,

"It happened to me as a child," "I don't know what came over me" or "It wasn't me"or just simply that "The child is telling a lie."

Jason is a good man, unwilling to believe that some humans may not be descendants of God. Oz, on the other hand has some how miraculously become the part of Jason that knows that all that breaths has not come from the bosom of God. For him there would be glory in taking the lives of such predators and, his revenge comes without remorse or guilt. Oz would do it with pride, but can only perform with Jason as his conduit to becoming matter.

Finally … after all the sleepless nights and Jason's dreams of the pleading children, his inert angel was able to take control. While within Jason, Oz has learned that he has very little recollection of his origins or what may be left of his angelic powers. He has also learned to suppress the disciplines that are instilled in an angel who can only perform the so-called good deeds.

Every day, Jason continues to live the life of a good man. He loves his family, he's hard working and he's filled with dreams of the world becoming a heavenly place very soon. In the eyes of his fellow men, he is far above average and an honor to know. At most times, he is also very humble.

Now, in his late night trances he is about to unleash Oz to answer the pleas of the children in his dreams. He is one man with a Godly gift of compassion, yet he is also at the same time one angry angel with the gift to respond with the vengeance of that very same God. He will avenge the helpless.

On this night, a four-year-old child named Eric, who was barely able to speak understandably, managed to reach up and actually grab one of Jason's fingers.

"That man threw me," he said in his childish voice. Ironically the child's touch opened Oz's eyes to another time and place. Oz entered the eyes of the child, and from Eric's eyes Oz looked into the face of a Boston man. The man smiled as he cradled Eric's just awakened body and held it over the rail of a six-story balcony. Eric's natural fear of falling caused his lips to quiver as he attempted to cling to the front of the man's shirt.

"Come on my little buddy, let go of me and enjoy your journey. This world is no place for a precious baby like you."

The man lowered his arms further over the rail as if to roll Eric off of his forearms. Eric held on tighter. In a panic, his entire mouth trembled exposing his chattering lower teeth. He now desperately clung to the only small piece of the man's shirt that was reachable.

The man kept yanking Eric's small hands away from his shirt, and all the while Eric was crying out in sounds that only the utmost fear could cause. He continued to cling to the man and hold on for dear life.

"Mommy!" he cried out.

"No, not mommy. I'm not your mommy."

He was not a mommy that was for sure; he did have a few kids of his own, which made him a father in the eyes of many. He was also a teller at the local bank, which made some folks assume he could be trusted.

In addition to his image of trust, he acted as a good neighbor, occasionally watching some of the children in the apartment building while their mothers went out. Now, he was in the process of covering up his ongoing sexual abuse and his most recent violent sexual attack that left Eric physically and visually injured.

Realizing he had over-performed his acts of sex and that there would be no way to hide it, he had become remorseful about what he'd just done and immediately wanted to repent of his sinful ways and start over.

He knew that it would be much too painful if his family found out and heaven forbid that his co-workers or friends got wind of his perversions. No, in order for him to cleanse himself and seek forgiveness from God he had to take his victim out of the equation and at the same time make it look like an accident.

"Just let go, my sweet little man. It will be over in a second and no one will ever know."

Oz now seemed to be looking directly into the man's face as he continued his attempt to shake Eric loose. His expression changed from a phony grin to a look of hatred and desperation as he was finally able to grip the child's body and hold him far enough away that there was nothing left for him to grab. With the child still trying to latch onto him and struggling, the man finally managed to toss Eric's body away from the railing and down to his death below.

Oz fell with the child, while looking into the man's face that was filled with evil and wore a half smile. The evil man leaned over the rail and watched as Eric and Oz descended to the ground. As Eric lay dying at Oz's feet, Oz leaned over and lifted him up into his arms. Eric whispered mommy once more before letting go of life.

Oz looked up at the man still peering down from above and roared like an animal on fire as his hatred and lust for revenge moved him into an uncontrollable state of fury. His instincts told him to scale the building while his blood was still boiling with anger and rip out the heart of the evil man. As he leaped up to the first balcony railing, his attention was drawn to a soft voice whispering to him in a calming manor.

"The child has passed on. What has happened cannot be changed. You have let him to tell his story. He may now rest in peace." The soft voice was somehow familiar to Oz and caused him to quickly drop back to the ground and turn his head upward looking for its source.

Though this angelic voice was calming, it was not enough to halt his fury.

"No!" he screamed. "I should have done something. Why did I have to watch like a helpless coward?"

"This event did not occur today. This taking of the child's life cannot in anyway be undone. Even our God cannot change what has already happened."

"Damn it! Why did you have to make me watch?"

"You are here and have seen of your own free will at the request of this child's spirit."

Every muscle in Oz's face was flexed with hatred and anger that as an angel he was not supposed to know. Again, he turned his head upward towards the man that was still strangely looking down, not at Eric's body but at Oz.

Oz was interrupted by another voice. This time that of policemen speaking to each other. Oz immediately wondered why the two policemen were unaware of him standing right next to them. Obviously they could not see him but it was just as obvious that the man above could.

"It looks like the kid somehow fell off the balcony."

"The poor kid never stood a chance of surviving a fall like this. While they determine the cause and time of death, let's see if we can find the mother."

The two officers proceeded into the apartment building and located the mother of the child. She had been fast asleep. She had been drugged by the man she thought was a friendly neighbor. She had known him since Eric was born.

Neither the mother nor the police were aware that the child had been sexually abused. It was assumed that the child wandered out onto the balcony and somehow fell off.

"This was simply a terrible accident — an open and shut case," one of the policemen said.

As the night went on, the news of what had happened quickly spread throughout the building. Among the gathered neighbors stood the man of the hour, pretending to find out what had happened along with his neighbors. The murderer was the first to lend his comforting arms to Eric's mother.

"What a terrible accident," the killer said.

Eric's mother responded by saying, "If I had only stayed awake, I could have stopped him. If I hadn't fallen asleep he would be alive. Oh my God, why? Why, God? Why? Why my baby? What did I do wrong?" The mother remorsefully repeated her questions to God again and again.

"It's going to be all right. He is with God now. He's in a better place. Jesus has already forgiven you. It was a horrible accident," he said.

The Boston man, George Hamm, had gotten away with murder. Three months later, George thought it was all behind him. Though he had gotten away with the crime, it wasn't enough. He still felt the threat of being exposed and going to prison.

He wanted to be a new man. No more yielding to his lust for innocent children. He wanted to start his life anew in another place. He packed up his family and moved. They settled into a high-rise apartment just outside of Pittsburgh where he was originally from. They had moved right into Oz's lap.

Once settled in, George could breath easy again knowing he had gotten away with murder. His ploy had been foolproof — use a trusting mother to get to the child, and then use the child for sexual satisfaction. Find away to make the child accept your acts then dispose of the child making it look like an accident. Finally, move on to the next victim after a short time of guilt.

He had even learned to ask God to forgive him and not let anyone know. Now that his fear of getting caught had passed, he it became clear to him that he was ready to seek another young boy.

This time there would be a problem. Oz knew about George … and against the will of God Oz had a plan of his own.

The Boston ordeal wasn't over for Oz, in fact it had just begun. Now it wouldn't end until Oz did the cleansing himself. George had gotten away with nothing, Oz would make sure of it. George would now become the prey.

Oz was a factor that predators, up until now, were unaware of. They were about to be introduced Oz's fury. Instead of being temporarily haunted by their own guilt, they would now become hunted by the likes of Oz.

†

"The serial killer has the same personality characteristics as the sex offender against children"

— Dr. Mace Knapp,
Nevada State Prison Psychologist

†

*"2/3 of all prisoners convicted of rape
or sexual assault had committed their crime against a child"*

— BJS Survey of state Prison Inmates, 1991

†

"Pedophilia appears to be a sickness of which there is no stop in place. When a person engages in this sort of activity an example should be set. When found guilty a temporary fix should be life imprisonment. As a permanent fix, my first inclination is to shoot 'em and have some one cut off a valuable part of his or her atomy, preferably the scrotum."

— Benjamin G. Ashe,
Businessman and retired police officer

CHAPTER TWO

A few months later:

George Hamm was sitting alone comfortably in his plush entertainment room watching a Monday night football game when his attention was drawn to a hard knock on his front door.

"Who is it?" he shouted.

"It's just me," answered Oz, in the soft and gentle voice of Jason.

"Who?"

"It's me, Oz." George opened the door as if he knew someone named Oz.

"What do you want?" he asked.

"How are you, George? I'm Oz and I came to talk to you about Eric."

Immediately George attempted to push the door shut while saying he didn't know any Eric. But Oz had placed his foot in the door opening preventing it from closing.

"Sure you do," Oz said while quickly forcing himself into the apartment. The quick push caught George off guard as he tripped backwards and stumbled onto the floor.

"What the hell are you doing pushing your way into my house?" he asked as he quickly jumped up onto his feet. By now Oz had pushed the door closed behind him and was calmly leaning against it.

"I came to talk to you about Eric," he repeated.

George paused with his fist balled up down at his side and postured in his "I'll kick your ass" position. "I said I don't know any Eric and I want you out my house before I get my gun and kill you mister!"

Oz responded in an even more calm voice. "Sure you do. You knew Eric; you knew him very well. You remember. He's the four year boy that fell off of a balcony a few months back."

George, still posturing and panting in a show of anger, seemed to be lost for words for a split second. Most cowards that intimidate their victims recognize a sense of fear when confronted by and adult male. Oz stood at over six feet tall and and had a gentle face, but his body was strong broad shouldered with thick forearms and thighs as strong as tree trunks.

"Number one, I don't know you and number two, I could shoot you for coming into my home without my permission."

"Cool down, George. I know you could do a lot of things but right now let's just talk about what you've already done," Oz said in a stern voice while holding his right hand up and opened it at the level of George's face.

"Why don't we talk and see if Eric is angry with you. He trusted you until he learned to fear your powerful dominance. He trusted you up until your tender touches of affection turned to something much more painful. He wanted to live and grow into a loving human.

"He wanted to remain here with his loving and trusting mother. He wanted to go to school and learn to play with other children his own age. He wanted to anticipate gifts, run as fast as the wind and someday maybe become a hero. Now he wants me to speak with you and assure you that you will not harm and disrupt another child's life for the sake of your own perverted pleasures."

"You're crazy. The police said he fell from the balcony. That means I had nothing to do with it."

"I know what the police said but I also know what you did. You see, I was there. I watched as he pleaded with you. I watched him cling to you. I saw you and your smiling eyes enjoying the power and arrogance of this position.

"You looked at Eric as a cheap toy before dropping him to his death. I even observed you taking a deep breath and releasing a sigh of relief that no one would find out about your overwhelming lust for helpless, trusting children."

"You're crazy. Get out of here right now!" George said as he retreated toward his bedroom as if going for a gun that he didn't have. Oz calmly followed him around, asking questions all the while.

"What's the matter, George? Are you angry that I know? Are you embarrassed? Are you scared? Do you think you might go to jail? Slow down, George, we've got a lot to talk about. Maybe we can discover ways to prevent this from happening to some of the many children that might suffer the same destiny."

"I told you to get out of my home mister!" he screamed while opening a drawer on his nightstand only to find Oz still in pursuit continuously asking question after question.

"George, what made you such a selfish and cold blooded man?"

George stopped pretending to find his gun and reached for the phone. "I'm calling the police."

"Go ahead, call them. Hurry up. Maybe they'll come here and find some of the photos you've got hidden inside your projector."

"You know what? I'm not calling anyone I'm just gonna kick your ass real good."

"Another bogus threat. Huh, George? No gun. No 911 call. No courage to kick anything but children. You poor man, you really believe that your ability to instill fear has made you god-like. It's not working with me, George I'm not afraid of you.

"So, we might as well get past this game of bully charades and proceed to an idea of what I should do about it for the sake of Eric and others like him. And even for the sake of others like you George."

George was nervously pacing around his bedroom while trying to think of what he was going to do next. Oz watched patiently, still wearing a slight smile of satisfaction; the satisfaction of knowing exactly what needed to be done.

"Where and when did you get the notion that you should prey upon helpless babies to fulfill your sexual needs? Where does it come from, George? I need to know. I've got all kinds of speculations of how it must start, but they are all just speculations.

"What made you such a man that you felt the need to do the unacceptable? Who introduced such a thought? Why is it so overwhelmingly tempting? Is it that reasoning never sets in? Where does the pleasure lie in it for you?

"Why not an adult women? Or is it that all of the above applies in addition to your special need to practice this godless cruelty? Questions, questions, questions — I have so many. Do you have any answers, George?

"Oh, and while I'm at it, why did you kill the child's body, wasn't killing his loving spirit enough? Again I ask, what pleasure do you get from it? Is it in the yielding to your self-image of a king-like prominence?

"Why is it that you so quickly yield to the temptation to touch a child when others are around but no one is looking? Or maybe it's that you are so inadequate and selfish and without manhood. Or better yet, is it that instilling that much pain and fear makes you feel special in your own mind?"

"I told you I want you out of my house. You're not a policeman. Who are you anyway? What's with all these questions that I don't have to answer? Just get out. Get out now!"

"Sorry, George. I can't leave. I've come to perform a duty and to fulfill a promise."

"Why did you come here, Ozzie or whatever your name is? Why don't you just get out before I—"

Oz interrupted, "Before you what, George? We've already gone through the fact that you're not going to do anything."

George stood dumbfounded, not knowing what to say next.

"George, my friend, I'm just going to come out and say it. I've come to get revenge for Eric's death," Oz said in a matter-of-fact way. "I've come to put you out of your misery."

George began to look around nervously for a way to escape. Oz intentionally took his eyes off George and gazed out of the only window in the room leaving the door as a potential exit for his prey. George jumped at the opportunity and ran for the door and out into the hall. While exiting he was yelling at the top of his lungs.

"Get out of my house! He's trying to kill me! He's trying to kill me!" he shouted. He ran to and frantically pushed the button for the elevator. When it didn't come fast enough, he ran to the exit door only to find it jammed.

By now, Oz had slowly entered into the hall about thirty feet from one of the elevator doors that had just opened. George ran inside, continuously yelling. Before Oz could get to the door, it closed. In George's haste of pushing elevator buttons, he acciden-tally pushed the button for the ninth floor roof terrace.

After stopping on each floor on its way up, the elevator door opened at the top and George franticly ran out onto the roof level. The elevator door closing behind him. With the number-one eleva-tor heading back down, George realized that the roof wasn't where he wanted to be. Oz had also reached the rooftop with the other elevator.

"Well, here we are again just the two of us. Me and you, George. Let's talk some more. Huh, George?" Oz jested.

George ran to the building's three-foot parapet wall. He stopped and looked over the ledge at the more than one hundred foot drop to the pavement below. "Leave me alone. You're crazy. Help, help!" he yelled to no avail while waving and trying to get the attention of someone in an adjacent building. He ran along the building's perim-eter trying to make his way to an exit of some sort.

Oz calmly stood and watched George run the whole roof deck until he was back standing near where he had started.

"Get away from me! I told you I didn't do anything to that boy. He fell off of the balcony. It was an accident."

"Look, George, I'll make you a deal — kind of-like a deal with the devil. You tell me why and what made you do it and I'll get on this elevator and you'll never see me again."

George momentarily stood still and pondered the proposition Oz had presented to him.

"Come on, Georg. Come clean. What made it acceptable for you? Why did you do it?"

"I don't know why," George finally broke down and blurted out.

"Are you driven by lust, George? Come on, talk to me. Don't make me give you your reasons, George. I want to hear it from you."

In a constantly whining voice George began his long list of reasons and whys. "I don't know. I didn't want to hurt him. I wanted to make love to him. I thought no one would ever know and I had no intention of hurting him. I was treating him lovingly and then something came over me and I lost control.

"After the thrill of lust was over and I'd found satisfaction, I realized what I'd done would ruin my life and I had no way to take it back. I had to do something … something so that I wouldn't go to prison.

"I was scared. I knew I'd messed up, but I couldn't help it. I didn't mean it. That overwhelming urge turned me into someone I'm not. It made me someone I could never be in my normal state of mind. I swear to you that I didn't know what I was doing.

"If you knew me, you'd know that I would never hurt anyone. Ask my friends, they'll tell you I'm well liked and fun to be around … I didn't mean it. I didn't mean it. Please help me. I'm so sorry."

"Stop it, George! Let's get back to reality. You sexually assaulted a four-year-old boy and when you feared someone might find out, you covered it up by making it look like the child fell off the balcony. And you know what else, George? I know that you've done it before *and* you plan on doing it again.

"Do you know why you'll do it again, George? Because you think you're good at it. You got away with it. It was so good for you, George, that you couldn't help it. You couldn't help it because of your own rotten self. Don't be sorry you did what you did, that means nothing to the child or his mother or any of us that care.

"Here's what to do, George. Be a hero … Go to edge of the roof, George, and jump. Save your family and your many friends the pain of knowing that they were deceived by a rotten excuse for a man.

Even better, George, don't jump. Let me throw you off. Then I'll be the hero that got rid of a self-centered pathetic coward who couldn't even stand up to his own sick and evil temptations. You should've sought help the moment the thought of touching a child crossed your mind, not after your pleasures had ended."

"But you said you would walk away if I told the truth."

"I *am* going to walk away, George, just as I said. It's just that you're not going to live to see me do it. You won't live to see another day or rape another child."

"You lied! What kind of man are you that your word doesn't stand for anything?"

"I'm the same kind of man that you are. I'm cunning, deceptive and cold-blooded."

Out of the blue the coward in George came bursting through. "No, don't kill me. I need help," he begged

"And that's what I've come to do — help you."

"No! Please, I can change."

"And you will. You're going to change from living to dying with Eric's and my compliments. You're a big man, George. Fight me off like you should've fought off your desire to tamper with babies.

"I'm going to end your stinking life. I guess I'm sick, too, George. I need help just like you and Eric did. And guess what? There's no one here to help me or you, George."

George began to run with nowhere to go. Oz simply stalked him slowly until he was cornered with no escape.

"Come on and fight George, save yourself. You know, even little Eric tried to cling to life because he knew he didn't deserve to die. If he were a little older or a little bigger he would've fought you to the end. Instead, he cried out for his mother."

George began to pant and muster up some anger. With both fists balled up at his sides he lowered his head and grunted like a bull. He had stopped begging and was now charging at Oz as if he was going to butt him with the top of his head. Oz side-stepped the attack and tripped George as he went by.

Oz taunted him to do it again. After a few reckless attempts, George slowly got up and attacked once again, this time raging and screaming blindly with his eyes closed. His attempt ended with him stumbling and tumbling over the edge of the roof's parapet. Somehow he managed to grab a small metal rail and it kept him from falling to the ground below.

"That was good, George. That showed your desire to live and to hold on to the only life available to you — the only life you've come to know. That was truly good. Now, see if you can pull yourself up. Come on, George. Pull up and save yourself"

"I can't … I can't pull myself up and I can't hold on."

"George, don't you dare let go! If you give up and fall, then I won't have done my part. Let me help you." Oz reached over and let George grab his shirtsleeve.

"I'm sorry, George, you're just too heavy for me to pull up. If you were only a child I could've been the one to save your life. Just like you said, I'm sorry for what I'm about to do."

While George grabbed and clung to save his own life, Oz grabbed George's shirt. Once again he taunted George, telling him to save himself. "Hold on, George. What ever you do, don't let go."

"No! Please don't let me fall." George was slowly losing his grip and there was nothing that Oz intended to do about it. In a further attempt to save himself, George scratched and clawed at Oz's forearms before finally beginning to slip.

"I think you're sorry for what you did, George, but it's only because you would like to live to violate another child. Sorry, George. Your life as you have come to know it is over." Oz watched as George fell downward, screaming until he met the concrete surface below.

When Oz peered down over the parapet, George's body was still jerking as if trying to recover and get up.

"What are you doing, Oz?" The soft and gentle voice that Oz slightly recognized spoke out again. *"You can't kill what George has become. He is only a small part of something that's much bigger than you. He is just one of the symptoms of a sickness that both men and women all over the world deny having."*

Sarcastically Oz responded in a strong and stern voice, "Well, not this one. This man, George, is now cured. He's not a symptom of anything anymore. As for the rest of them, well … we shall see what we can do. As long as blood runs through this man's veins, I will without a doubt satisfy the voices of these abused babies. They will have their day of reckoning."

The angelic voice continued on as Oz headed home to become Jason.

Jason woke up late the next morning with no memory of what, if anything, had actually happened. Both Helen and Sissy had already gone to their prospective obligations for the day. He gave himself a hardy stretch and yawn and then sat for a moment on the side of the bed wondering why after such a long night's sleep he was feeling more tired than usual. Jason stood up and noticed unexplainable scratches on both of his forearms.

"Damn," he said to himself. "How in the hell did I get all scratched up like this?" Before he could give it any more thought the phone rang.

"Hello, honey," he said after reading Helen's name on the Caller ID.

Helen responded, "Hi, honey, how was your trip?"

He didn't know what she was talking about. He wanted to ask her, what trip? Jason was puzzled but remained silent for a split second before finally responded by saying, "Fine … my trip … was fine."

Helen babbled on about some things Sissy and she had to do and what they had done while he was gone. Jason listened, but didn't really hear a word she said. After hanging up, he sat back down on the bed and attempted to make sense of his blank mind.

He was totally clueless about what had happened before he woke up this morning. That is … other than the fact that he thought he'd caught up on the much-needed sleep he so badly wanted.

Yet, now that he had talked to Helen, he was suspicious that he might somehow be losing his mind. He looked at the clock. It was 2:30 p.m. and he remembered going to bed at 9:00 p.m. the previoust night. The problem was, the day on the clock. It should have read, Monday at 2:30 p.m. instead it read as Wednesday. *Did I sleep for three days more than I can remember? What did I do for two days that I don't remember?*

Another two weeks of pleasant family life went by without any nightmares or sleeplessness nights on Jason's part. However, Oz was awake while Jason slept. He had listened to every voice in the room — every child that had a story to tell. Each time Jason went into the slightest sleep deep enough for him to become active, Oz sympathized with the children.

Then, one Saturday afternoon while sitting in front of his computer, Jason found himself dozing off and Oz found himself tuning in. By way of a breaking news story projected on the computer screen, Oz was informed that the body of a four-year-old girl had been found. She appeared to have drowned and had washed ashore in Daytona Beach, Florida.

The child's name was Maria. How the child got there and the cause of her death had yet to be determined. Oz knew her name, the cause of her death, and how she died. He even knew her killer.

The newscaster revealed the color of the clothes the child was wearing in addition to the girl's approximate age in an attempt to locate the her parents or someone with information about her. There were no reports of a missing child anywhere in the area.

The first thought was that this may be another one of those cases that would never be solved unless someone stepped forward, which in these kinds of cases was unlikely. When a child ends up in the Atlantic Ocean in the middle of spring, it usually indicates an attempt to dispose of a murdered body.

The young victim was the daughter of a heavily drug addicted twenty-six-year-old Italian woman who lived in the nearby suburbs. Maria had been physically abused almost daily by the mother for past three months and had been sexually abused even on her last day of life by the mother's forty-five-year-old pedophile friend and drug dealer.

The boyfriend, Montel, solved some of the unwelcome crying problems that occurred during his sexual escapades by injecting the little girl with small amounts of heroin. On this night, he went too far and she died from an overdose.

He made his case by convincing her mother they would both go to jail after the police had the chance to investigate the child's sexually abused body. Together they decided what to do with the corpse.

The couple placed her in a plastic bag filled with stones. They waited until the beach was nearly empty of people and took her out as far as they could into the ocean and dropped her to the ocean floor, hoping that she would never be found.

As they scurried away without looking back the impact of the incoming tide immediately tore the bag open and separated the child from the stone-filled bag. Unsuspecting and ironically in this case, the child had survived all of the abuse and the fatal drug injection but ultimately drown after struggling and gasping for air until she could no longer stay afloat.

Her body was later spotted by a shoreline fisherman, who then called the authorities. The couple had told all of their unconcerned but inquisitive associates that they'd sent the child to Texas to be raised by the woman's mother. The night after the child's death, they returned home and celebrated their independence by indulging themselves and friends with as much heroin as they could afford.

A few days later, after the local news had revealed that her body was found, Montel found himself walking along Daytona Beach looking for the plastic bag he had placed the child in. He was afraid that in his haste and thinking she would never be found, he might've left his fingerprints on the plastic bag.

He thought that if the bag was found, the police suspect it was a murder instead of the accidental drowning he had tried to make it seem. Their coverstory was also in danger of causing suspicion because they'd told their friends the lie Maria had been sent to Texas to her grandparents, and now she was dead and her body was found in Florida.

Night was about to fall as Montel walked along the peaceful shoreline. Even though his soul was filled with rot and he was up to no good, the sound of the sea and the beauty of the starlit night gave him a sense of serenity.

"Just like this beautiful night, life is also beautiful," he said to himself.

He had walked much further than he thought but he didn't seem to mind. He was a successful drug dealer that seldom got the opportunity to enjoy the natural things in the world.

"Life is good and beautiful," he said again.

Suddenly a soft voice interrupted Montel's blissful moment.

"Hello, Montel" Oz spoke with a slight indication of affection.

"Do I know you? You look familiar," Montel responded.

"No, you don't know me. But you and I know some of the same people."

Oz wore sunglasses to conceal the fact that his eyes were a glaring burnt orange color. Other than that, Oz appeared to be just another ordinary man.

"Hello, Montel," another voice greeted him from behind. Before he had the chance to identify the first voice, Montel turned around to face the other man that ironically also wore sunglasses on this moonlit night.

"And just who are you?" Montel asked in a matter of a fact way.

"I don't know the gentleman you're talking to but I do know more about you than I'd like to admit," the second man said. The second man, an angel named Jax, continued to speak in a light-hearted philosophic fashion with a cold edge.

"You know, you're right about how much beauty the world has to offer with all of its majestic views and natural gifts to mankind. I heard you say a moment ago in your own words that 'life is beautiful.' You know I've always said that for those who take a moment notice, the wonders of the world are just that and more.

"I'd like to take a walk with you for a moment, if you don't mind. And Mr. Oz, I don't know you or why you're here with him but I suggest you leave now. Mr. Montel and I have to discuss an issue about a murdered child."

"I appreciate your concern for me but for now I think I'll tag along. You see, I too have an issue with Mr. Montel," said Oz."

Montel began to impatiently and rudely babble about the things he had to do and that he really did't have time to walk around gawking at the world with two fools.

"Just for a short walk," Jax said. "That's all I'm asking of you Montel; just one moment of your valuable time. And I promise you, it won't be boring. Come on, what do you say?"

Montel, ignoring Jax's request, had already turned around and was heading back toward his car that was parked about a mile down the beach. Both Oz and Jax walked hurriedly behind him.

"Stepping up his pace and his subject matter, Jax said, "I don't want to waste a lot of your time but I'm trying to learn why men do the things that they do to women and children."

"Are you high on something man? You two better get the f—k away from me."

"You must remember the five-year-old named Seth up in Erie a few years back, and the four-year-old Maria that you recently dumped into the ocean?"

"What the hell are you talkin' about, fool?" Montel's face quickly turned pale as he realized something was not right. He began to walk away much faster than before, heading in the direction from which he'd come.

Oz quickly walked along trying figure out just who this Jax character was and why he was interfering with his attempt to get revenge for Maria

"No, Montel, don't run. Stay here and chat with me about how great the world is. I want to hear it," said Jax.

"I don't know you, man, and I've got to get back to my business."

"Why? Haven't you helped enough people get hooked on drugs while you position yourself to rape their babies? Did you kill Maria? Did you know that the child drowned not more than a couple of yards from where we are walking right now? I can almost hear her cry for help as we speak."

"I don't know what you're talking about." Montel stuttered out with fear in his voice while looking side to side as if deciding which way he should now begin to run.

"You know what I'm talking about. You know exactly what I'm talking about. Were you planning on drowning the child? Were you going to try and cover up your sexual abuses with the life of another helpless victim? Come on, you can tell me," Jax taunted.

"I don't know what you're talking about. I didn't kill anybody."

"Stop the lie!" Jax snapped while quickly turning his head towards Montel. "Stop the bull shit, I was there, I watched you drug and rape the child while the mother had nodded out from your drugs. I looked into your glorified eyes as you reached your sexual ecstasy."

"No, I don't want to hear this. It was not me, I swear to you in the name of God." His tone of voice had quickly changed. He was beginning to make his plea. In his mind he just knew that this man Jax had a gun; he wasn't sure why the other man, Oz, was there. They apparently didn't know each other but neither seemed to be there on his behalf. Other than that, how could he be so bold as to accuse him of what he knew he had done? Further more, how in the world could he know?

"I see," said Jax. "You want to use God as your witness. I've given Him the blame on many occasions myself. That won't work. You see God didn't inject her with drugs or rape her, you did. And believe me you don't want to bring Him in on this. This is between you and me"

"But, he didn't stop me."

"Make up you mind, did you kill her or not." Jax calmly asked. "Are you saying it was God and not you? I didn't see God there I saw you." During the conversation Jax had slowed Montel down and had been slowly edging him into the shallow waters along the shoreline.

"Where are you taking me?" asked Montel.

"Oh … we're just walking and talking. Isn't it a pretty night it's a little chilly but its still a great night isn't it? It's just like you were saying to yourself a moment ago. Look at the stars twinkling, the moon is shining and lighting a pathway just for us to walk along," Jax said, all of the while pointing to the moons reflection of light on the surface of the water. "Let's just walk you, me and Mr. Oz, who may leave any time he wishes. Let's talk about the evil things you've done to children." They were nearly up to their knees in the cool ocean water.

"I don't want to walk in the water, I can't swim." Montel said.

"I know," responded Jax. Montel had no idea why he continued to walk along beside Jax and Oz; he just blindly followed them.

"I'm going home. I don't have to listen to you. Who are you anyway? Are you the police?"

"No, I'm not a police officer Montel. My name is Jax and I've come to answer your prayers. I've come to help you be forgiven. "

"What do you mean?" Montel asked. Montel was transforming from a macho drug dealer into a frighten coward. He was walking where he didn't want to walk. Talking to a man he didn't want to talk to and unknowingly going to a place where he belonged.

"I'm going back to the shore," Montel said.

"No, Montel, you're not going back. Something tells me that you already know that," Oz finally spoke.

"I'm going home. I don't want to walk with you guys anymore." Signs of the brave acting drug dealer kept trying to break through and take over the situation to no avail.

"No Montel, it's all over. There's no one here for you to show off for. No ones going to cheer you on or give you a high five or give you your much needed false sense of being respected … It's time now for you meet your maker," said Oz.

"What are you trying to do? You have no authority over me."

"Nor you over her," responded Oz. "You took the authority against their will. Their lives and their happiness meant absolutely nothing to you. All you thought about was reaching a forbidden orgasm."

"You don't know what you're talking about. Tthere is nothing forbidden about sex." Montel's arrogance came and went from word to word while they talked. Both Oz and Jax paused for a moment after being caught off guard by Montel's statement.

Oz quickly rebounded. "So you think there is nothing wrong with raping a four-year-old and a five-year-old and then murdering them?

"Their deaths were accidental. I didn't intentionally kill ether one of them. I said, there is nothing forbidden about sex. It happens all the time. The mothers knew about it. God knew about it, I'm sure. No one cared. It was just a part of life. It goes on everywhere all of the time."

"I see," said Oz. "But here's the truth of the matter. It doesn't go on all the time and most of us *do* care. It's not a chosen part of these children's lives; it's a part that you have chosen for them. And, as far as the accidental murders that you mentioned go, I do understand because it seems that Mr. Jax is about to become a part of an accidental murder, too."

Montel's taunting statements had come to an end. Now he was coming back to his senses and was back to being afraid that he was about to be killed by two strangers.

"What do you two have to do with it? They weren't your children, they were mine. What gives you the right to try and kill me?" Montel asked in the voice of a reasonable man.

"Because just like you; we're taking the right to kill. Just like you needed to satisfy your needs, we need to satisfy ours. Unlike you, we will be taking the life of a man that deserves to die. No one should care that you won't be around — you're a dangerous child rapist," Oz said, assuming that Jax felt the same way.

"Guess what, Mr. Oz and Mr. Jax ... I don't care. I don't know why I've walked out here with you but I'm not going any further. In fact, I'm going home right now and I suggest that you don't try to stop me. I don't think you could really kill a man over children that weren't yours. I don't feel good about what happen but you can't prove that I did anything, so good night to both of you assholes. I hope I never see either of you again."

"I see, now you've made up your mind. There is no remorse or regret on your part. It wasn't a bad thing to you. To you it was just another day in the life of a drug dealing pedophile," said Jax.

"Look at me, I'm not, as you say 'just a drug dealer', I'm also a junkie. Who would convict a junkie? They'll say that I'm sick. I might finally understand that what I did was wrong, but I'm not sure of what I may have done while I was high. I need help getting off the drugs that might have caused me to do some of the things that were done."

"Of course no one will convict you, but little Maria already has. Me? Well, hell, I'm just as crazy as you are. I'm going to smile while you're getting there. I'm going to smile while the water rushes over your head. I'm going to enjoy pushing you away as the sea finds its way up into your brain and down into your cold, wicked heart.

"I want you to think of Maria the whole time. In fact, forget the bullshit, Montel! I'm done talking to you. I could go on and on but there's no need. You already know the victims of your so-called love and affection, and you have a drug habit to blame it all on. You know what, Montel? I love you just like you loved them."

The water was now just below Montel's shoulders with each wave rushing water up into his face.

Jax again changed the subject. "Isn't the world a place of great beauty? Look at all the stars the sky. Well, it just takes my breath away … kind of like the water will do as it rushes into your mouth and nostrils. Isn't the water breathtaking, Montel? … Isn't it?"

"Stop this shit!"

Montel was a strong-headed man sold on the fact that there was nothing wrong with what he did. And if there was, he figured it could all be blamed on the drugs. Montel was treading water for the first time in his life and the realization that he might be about to drown was upon him.

"Okay," he said with his first sign of panic. "I'll n-n-never do it again … I'll confess. Just get me b-b- back on s-s-s-olid g-g-ground," he said while swallowing seawater between each word he spoke.

"Oh, don't agonize I'm not going to let you die, Montel," Jax said and paused as the three were forced to tread water because the ocean floor had dropped away. Montel was now panicking and paddling harder to try to save his life.

Jax continued, "I'm going to personally kill you. Oh … and don't worry, you're going to just the place you deserve." Jax looked directly into Montel's eyes and smiled.

"You're not my first, you know. Nor will you be my last."

"No! Please. You can't just kill me. I'm a child of God!" Montel looked over at Oz with a pleading expression on his face.

"Isn't it a beautiful night?" Oz said, copying Jax's careless attitude.

"No, I don't like this night."

"Why not? Look at the stars and how they sparkle. I just love talking about my Father's creations. Look at the moon. It seems to be hanging there just for the three of us. I've often wondered why folk say, 'You can see a man's face in the moon if you look closely.'

Me, I only see that gorgeous glow. It reminds me of people who are good at heart. When I pass them on the street, they to seem to have a glowing aura about them. That illumination is the certain glow of love. You, on the other hand, seem to be projecting a certain gloom. Sometimes you and men like you are so morally bankrupt that you omit sounds of crying children or heartbeats coming to a stop, or voices of a pleading child. Why, it's no wonder you don't like the sparkle of the moonlit night.

Look out into the horizon, Montel. Here, let me help you a little so you can see. See how the water's surface sparkles. Out on the horizon it appears to be calm, and yet … here around you it's horrifyingly active and chaotic as if it wants to swallow you up and spit you into hell."

"Please, help me. Please, please, forgive me! I am a child of God. Oh God, please help me."

"No, no there'll be no help for you, other than me. I'll help you find the peace you deserve."

"Okay, I'm s-saying … I'm … s- sorry for e-everything."

"Of course you are, now. Being sorry is *not* enough. Maria wants the comfort of knowing you will never create fear again. That you will never again confuse a child by plotting to rape and kill an innocent soul."

"I'm afraid of water," he said in a cowardly voice.

"Oh, come on, the water is barely up to your neck. In a moment it will be well over your head. Let's just enjoy our walk. Who knows, maybe someone will come to your rescue."

Both Oz and Jax had removed their sunglasses revealing a harsh glaring coldness that told Montel it was too late. Jax held his mouth tilted with a slight smile. His voice sometimes sounded like that of a friend attempting to persuade another into a devilish adventure. He taunted the man.

"Try and be brave while you are dying. I'll be right here by your side. We'll keep talking. Would you like to keep talking? How about this, yeah though we walk through the valley of the shadow of death. I shall fear no evil for I am with you.

"Please … I-I-I don't want to die."

"Why do you keep saying the same thing again and again? 'I don't want to die! I don't want to die!' Stop it!" Jax shouted. "Stop it and be the bold and outspoken man you were about ten minutes ago when you were talking about 'there's nothing wrong with sex with a child.' I found a lot wrong with it. No one will even know your dead other than us. This will be our secret. Now let us enjoy your ride into hell. I owe it to all of those young children whose lives have been shortened by people like you."

"I'm s-s-sick I n-n-need help. You've got to see that k-k-killing even me is wrong." Now Montel was in a full panic, splashing with one hand and trying to cling to the now torn shirt of Oz. His head suddenly went deep under the surface as he let go of Oz and struggled to get back above water on his own.

"P-p-p-please, help me," he begged as he sank a little.

"P-p-please."

Suddenly Jax lifted Montel up out of the water from just below his armpits.

"Thank you. Thank you so much." Montel said as he forced the ocean water from his mouth and nose. After lifting Montel as high as he could he shoved him into the air and further out towards the deeper sea.

"Bye, Montel. Don't thank me. I'm just making sure you have the time to realize and enjoy the feeling of the death that is sucking the air from your chest. But I am sure that those helpless kids are thanking me. In fact I'm thanking you for the pleasures of watching you fight the mighty sea for your life or should I say beg.

"I'm going to leave you now. If you stop splashing you will have few a moments of peace before God's merciless ocean swallows you up and spits you into the lap of hell … maybe there you will be forgiven and the fire won't be so hot for so long. Who knows maybe you'll like it. The possibility of you being in heaven scares me. Goodbye, Mr. Montel. I know I'll be seeing remnants of you through out my journey but none of the others will be you as you were."

With that last statement Oz and Jax turned and walked to shore never looking back. Once on the beach they both lay down onto their backs and talked of things they had in common as they gazed up into the sky.

The soft voice from somewhere that seemed to follow Oz to his victims found this an appropriate time to speak to both of them.

"How do you feel, Oz? How do you feel, Jax? You've taken it upon yourselves to take another life."

"Actually I feel great because I know the number of lives that I have just saved," said Oz.

"I see … so what gives you the right to play the Almighty?"

"This has nothing to do with God. This is about men — men that kill and are killed on behalf of God. Jjealousy, lust, selfishness, greed — you name it — they will all kill for it. And more times than not, even entire nations will go to war and kill for the sake of this kind of dominance.

"The consequence of killing is often rewarded. We have a motive to kill. There are diseases of the mind that have run amuck among a certain kind of man. There are men that are working diligently to convince the world that trampling the spirits of women and children should be accepted."

"So what do you plan on doing? Are you taking it upon yourself to become some sort of child savior or liberator?"

"Well, I hadn't really thought of it in that way but the answer is yes. I, or we, would like to be a part of the cure. We'd like to open the eyes of real men and bring into their hearts an obsession to stand up and fend for the rights of sexually abused children. The consequence of rape has always been and should remain death."

"So, do you plan on personally killing every man that rapes a child?"

Jax quickly answered yes.

Oz pondered the question, then said, "Yes, if it is possible. ... Yes, that would be my answer."

"And what of the fact that you are a mortal and you stand to be overwhelmed by the sheer number of child molesters that exist in your city alone? What of the fact that you might be arrested or killed by a predator? You must know that they are not all going to just lay down and die for you."

"Then they should spread the word that some men are standing tall and are willing to die for the sake of one another and the well-being of our children."

"But they shall also spread the word to those that justify their actions and believe that they have a God-given right to pursue their own worldly pleasures and desires; they might be willing to kill the likes of you if you interfere."

"We will rely upon the instincts of the many caring mothers to stand vigilant over their own and the children of others, until the pedophile sickness is put to rest. In the mean time, I, or we, will be cause for concern."

Oz's own voice of reasoning was losing the battle of what was right and wrong. Oz mumbled and ended the conversation with his own words of, "So be it."

"I concur," stated Jax and bid Oz farewell as he walked away.

A couple of days later back in Pittsburgh, Jason, still obliviously unaware of Oz's wayward nighttime activity, continued his typical day-to-day life. Inevitably his subliminal conscience stirred concerns about the growing problem of child abuse.

One Sunday morning he asked Helen what she thought should be done with child abusers.

She responded, "I think they should cut off their wieners and put them into prison with violent criminals who are gay. Why do you ask?" Of course Jason knew that some child molesters are female and without penises. The idea of cutting off the penis is the number-one quoted solution. Unfortunately it is also known that it would not stop a pedophile from doing what his perverted mind has told him to do. The conversation about child abuse was always avoided in Jason's household, as it is in many households where it existed or still does exist.

Helen continued, "It seems to be something that has gotten worse over in resent years. I read that gays and lesbians who were previously considered no threat to children or have been discovered in many cases to be the very root of the cause. I can see why that may make sense. Sex is the essence of the way that some determine their gender. It kind of indicates that there are no limits to the importance of the sex act if you can choose your gender based upon a passing desire to perform an act and call yourself a third or fourth different gender.

"I can easily see how given access to children, they might very well encourage the openness to pursue every lustful yearning as a true sexual identity. They might even encourage, by example, that gender is determined not by genitals but by the sexual acts that one craves to experience.

"I have a friend who made a funny but commonsense statement that went something like this: He says that even if he enjoyed having sex with a tree and began to crave that tree every time that he became lustful, he would still be a male because of his penis. He went on to say that, under gay terms he could possibly be called a tree f — ker and be designated as another gender despite the fact that tree f — king would not change his maleness.

In other words, my understanding of what he is saying is this: if you have a penis no matter what you chose to do with it, nothing changes your gender. It seems that this type of argument has made a lot of gays and lesbians bitter enough to impose their convictions upon children to the point that they have become an active part of the molestation disease just to prove a point.

"Their point being that they were born as the opposite gender and should not have to live with it. Thus, children are fair game because according to some that's when their true sexual preference is being decided, if that could possibly be something that can be decided. I think that the suggestion that being gay or lesbian is acceptable may influence young minds or at lease cause questions as to which of the four options above are they. When in reality there are only two. No matter how sexually creative one gets, you still remain the gender you were born with, i.e. male or female, or hey … maybe tree f — kers," she jokingly said.

"I thought you believed in gay and lesbian rights."

"I do, when the fulfillment of their sexual fantasies and desires is with other consenting adults and not being imposed as a third and fourth gender. But obviously they can be just as devious towards children and vulnerable persons as heterosexuals. In addition, the majority of sexually abused children are boys and the majority of child sexual abusers are men. Do you get it? These are males desiring males. I believe that makes it a homosexual act. Sexual abuse doesn't seem to have age or gender boundaries."

"You may be right but it would be sad to think that a sex act could become a pivoting point that's more important than the well-being of children and it's certainly nice to know that for most of us there is more to life than finding a place to reach an orgasm."

Ironically before Jason could finish giving his opinion about gay and lesbian rights he looked down at an article that was in the Pittsburgh Post; about a baby less than two years old that had been abused and murdered by her own father.

"Wow," he said, listen to this. "There was a man over in nearby Braddock that was arrested for murdering his daughter who was about to turn two years old. It says here that he confessed to leaving his daughter out in the cold to freeze to death. Here's his confession. Quote:

> Y'all dudes are excellent; I don't feel like you guys are trying to pressure me. Y'all been good to me … I woke up about 3: am on the morning in question and went down into the basement. I started drinking brandy, and then she came down into the basement. I was frustrated with her to keep tearing up them pampers,' he said 'I told her 'Boonie, stop, stop, stop! You got to stop this.'
>
> As soon as I sent her up stairs, she came back down. I was so mad she kept tearing up the pampers.' When she wouldn't listen, I kicked her between her legs and she started to bleed. I tried to make it stop with a tee shirt, a towel and my finger. I got scared. 'I wrapped her up in a blanket. I wrapped her up real tight, and I put on my coat and walked out the front door.

I stood there for a second. I was crying and she was crying. And I thought I would put her up by the sewer, and then I just said no. I started walking down the tracks. I was thinking where am I gonna put her at? Then I put her down with the blanket around her. I wrapped it again, tight enough so if she did get up she had to work her way out of that blanket

She was cryin', man. She was cryin'. I started cryin'. I just took off down the tracks and went home. I left her in the weeds. I walked a short distance away and listened to her cry for ten minutes. I kept telling her how sorry I was 'cause I *was* sorry. That I am, I am sorry.

"During his testimony, the detective said a child's footprints led to the spot where Nyia's body was found," Jasons said. "The father never explained why he left his daughter out in the cold wearing nothing but a sweater and a diaper."

"Wow, that's just unbelievable. It makes my stomach hurt just to think what that baby had to go through. That bastard needs to die," Helen said while shaking her head in disbelief.

Even mild mannered Jason agreed with Helen — that bastard needs to die.

Jason was visibly disturbed by the article to the point that he got up from his chair and walked into his bedroom without another word to Helen. After closing the door he leaned against the wall and placed his tearful eyes against his forearm.

"Damn it, damn it, damn it! That bastard needs to die," he painfully whispered. "Why didn't we do something to stop him?" Jason was torn but something inside of him was furious.

"Are you all right, honey?" Helen asked without opening the door. "Can I come in or do you want to be left alone?" she asked.

"Please, just give me a moment alone. I don't know what's wrong. I guess that article threw me a little. I'll be okay. I need do digest how and why I'm taking it so hard. It's like I should've done something about it even though I know I couldn't have."

"Well, you just holler if you need me, honey I'll be right here. Oh, and honey … I know that if you could've done anything you would have."

Even those words of encouragement from Helen, Jason knew something was going on inside his mind that could not be that easily harnessed. That baby was speaking to him loud and clear and Jason wanted to talk to the man that cold-bloodedly raped and murdered his own two-year-old daughter because, according to him, she wouldn't stop taking off her pamper. *What sense does any of this make? Is he lying?*

Something inside of Jason was at work, telling him that it had nothing to do with frustration from diaper changes. It had more to do with a perverted and overriding lust for sex. That the man was helplessly trapped by his own empty mind; so much so that he committed the God-forbidden act. Something else inside of Jason asked, *Does the reason matter? The child has been cruelly and mercilessly murdered by her father.* These thoughts were too much for Jason.

"Honey?" he called out, "I'm all right, you go ahead and head out. I'm going to lie down and rest for a while."

While Jason slept, Oz awakened. He found himself walking downtown along Pittsburgh's Grant St.

"Excuse me, sir. You can't urinate in public," a policeman instructed Oz. "Let me see some identification."

"I'm sorry, I don't have any," Oz responded.

"If you don't have any I.D. I'm going to have to take you in and book you for urinating in public, sir."

"Sorry, I don't have any."

Within an hour, Oz found himself inside the county jail and it wasn't even 7:30 in the evening. He was scheduled to be arraigned at 6 a.m. the next morning.

Oz had less than twelve hours to make his way into solitary confinement where Mr. Garret Watts was held and awaiting his sentencing. The solution was easy; he simply refused to enter his cell and caused enough ruckuses to be thrown into solitary confinement area. Once there, he was lucky enough to be in the cell right next to Mr. child murdering Watts himself …and it wasn't even 9 p.m.

After getting settled into his cell, he went right to making contact with his neighbor. "Hey, you in the next cell. What are you in here for?"

At first Mr. Watts didn't answer, so Oz went on talking. "I'm in here for nothing. You know, sometimes those folks out there make mistakes and don't realize that we do things we're not really responsible for. Sometimes things just go wrong and there are no explanations that they will ever understand. You know what I mean?" Still there was no response from Garret.

Oz wasn't about to give up. "Hey, man, I'm in here with you. We're in the same boat. Talk to me. Maybe we can help each other get through this."

Bingo … he spoke. "Man, I didn't do it."

"Do what, brother? What are you in for?"

"They said I killed my little girl but I'm tellin' you now, I didn't do it. I was drinkin' and I drank so much brandy I passed out. But I would never kill my own kid. You know what I mean, man?"

"Yeah, I hear you. So … who killed her, Garret?"

"I don't know, man … somebody. I just know it wasn't me."

"Who raped your baby, Garret?"

"I don't know, man. All I know is it wasn't me. Now, I might do time for something I didn't do. Man, this is a drag. You know what I mean?"

"Yeah, I hear you. So … what if I told you I'd like to kill the man that did it."

"I don't know who did it, man. I'm sitin' in here because I told them something I had seen on the news and they believed I did it. I don't belong in here. You watch, they'll find out who did it and then I can get out of here … You know what I mean?"

"Yeah, I hear you. So … can I tell you this? I know who did it." There was no response to that last statement. "Would you like me to kill him for you, Garret?" Still, there was no response. "Your baby, who you seem to not be that concerned about, has told me who did it. I think this guy deserves to die a horrible death. What do think, Garret?" Still, there was no response.

"Hey, listen, Garret. I'll make you a deal. If you'll help me kill the man that raped and killed your baby, I'll make sure you'll be set free."

"How do you know who did it, man?"

"Your daughter told me."

After a long silence Oz spoke again. "I don't have all night, Garret. Do you want to help me kill him or not?"

"How we gon'na get out?"

"I can get us out. I have a plan. Are you with me or not?"

"Yeah, just get me out."

"Now you're talkin', brother. Listen, we resemble each other enough; after they come down to give us a walk out on the tier this is what we'll do. When we return I'll walk into your cell and you walk into mine. Early in the morning they'll take you up for arraignment and you'll be set free. When they realize they've made a mistake they'll set me free too. They'll be looking for you everywhere, so here's what you do. Do you know the big sewer outlet not far from where he killed your baby?"

"Yeah."

"They'll never look there. You wait there for me and I'll pick you up and I'll take you to the guy that really did it. Then you can use my car to go somewhere and hideout until everything is cleared up. What do you think?"

"Man, I got'ta try something. I can't be goin' to prison for some thing I didn't do."

"Don't worry, I can guarantee you that you won't be going to prison under any circumstance. So, what do you say? Are we going to do it or not?"

"Yeah, man, get me out of here."

"When you get out just walk the bike path behind the jail past Hazelwood until you get under the Braddock Bridge, then you know where to go from there."

Everything went off as if were controlled from above. A murderer walked away from the county jail. Oz was released not long after and used someone's parked bike to get to Garret. Oz was worried that Garret would deviate and go off somewhere different, but when he arrived at the mouth of the sewer pipe down near the railroad tracks in Braddock there Garret was waiting patiently as instructed. It had just begun to snow and neither of them was dressed for the cold temperature.

"Damn, man, I thought you weren't goin' ta show up. It's cold as a bitch out here."

"I wouldn't have missed this for the world," Oz responded.

What had been referred to by Garret as a sewer pipe was really a six foot round concrete storm outlet that open up into the river below the railroad tracks. On the outer wall of the concrete pipe were embedded U-shaped metal rods used to hoist the pipe in place during construction. It was cold — very cold — andthe forecast called for it to get colder with snow as the day went on.

"Have you ever been down here before?" he asked Garret.

"I've been near here. Lets get out of here, it's creepy and it stinks."

"Look at all the empty brandy bottles there above the waterline in the grass. Isn't that the kind of brandy you drink, Garret?" Oz asked. By now Oz had walked around Garret to a point of having him trapped with the pipe and the hillside at his back. Garret began to get uneasy and thought that Oz might be up to no good. He began to slowly attempt to climb the slippery and lightly snow-covered hill behind him as they talked.

"What's wrong with you, man? I thought you were going to help me get away from here?"

"I am," said Oz. "I'm going to help you get as far away from here as you can possibly get. Isn't this where you brought your daughter's nine-year-old brother to have sex with him this past summer?" Oz asked.

Garret began to panic as his pin-sized mind finally confirmed that this wasn't what it appeared to be. He finally realized that Oz wasn't just a helpful fellow criminal. As he reached the halfway point up the hillside, he slipped and tumbled back down hitting his head on the concrete pipe and finally came to a stop right at Oz's feet. He was knocked out cold.

Oz used the shirt Garret was wearing to tie him tightly to the metal ring protruding from the pipe and patiently waited for him to regain consciousness.

"Well, your back with me," he said as Garret began to move and look around. "For a moment there I thought you were going to try to back out of our deal."

"Why am I tied up? Are you crazy or something?"

Oz kind of chuckled and answered, "No, I'm not crazy or nothing. Actually, I'm kind of satisfied with the way things have gone so far today."

"Yes, you are. You're crazy. Untie me you crazy bastard." Garret began to squirm and pull at the pieces of cloths that bound him.

Oz chuckled again and said, "I can't believe that you're calling me crazy, when you're the one that raped and killed your own baby. I'm not the one who's crazy here, Garret. I may be a little judgmental, as you can see, but crazy I am not."

"I didn't kill her, she froze. I was crying just like she was. I was scared and didn't know what to do." Surprisingly, Garret's voice had calmed down and he was speaking in a gentle way as if he truly weren't to blame.

"I'm sure you were scared. She was afraid too, Garret, but only after you left her here to die. You were afraid of being caught, just like all of the other snakes like you. It's over, Garret. You can lay here for a while and listen to your own tales. Who knows, maybe you'll believe that you didn't do it. It won't matter to me or your daughter."

"Don't leave me here; I want to go back to jail."

"Well, maybe if you scream loud enough someone will hear you. Oh yeah, you already know you can't be heard way down here. Don't you?" Oz turned and started to walk away when he realized that this would be a good time to fulfill the lie Garret had told to hide the fact that he had penetrated his daughter with his penis while he was in a violent rage, causing her to bleed badly.

Garret had stated in his confession that, "The baby kept taking off her pamper, so got angry and kicked her hard between her legs in an attempt to make her stop taking it off." He had stated that it was his kick that caused the baby to bleed and that he was just trying to stop the bleeding before he panicked.

Oz walked back to Garret and kicked him three times with all of his might. "Now I'm sure that's going to make you bleed. I wish I had the time to watch you freeze to death here where you've found so many moments of pleasure but I'm pretty sure that you want to be alone for you final orgasm. So … I bid you farewell and I hope you enjoy your journey."

As Oz topped the hillside about fifty yards from Garret, he turned around and looked back at his victim. He realized that Garret was no longer afraid and that he had not truly begged for his life as Oz had expected he would. In fact, Oz thought for a moment that while walking away he had heard or maybe just felt the bone-chilling sound of laughter.

Garret was simply laying there in a daze. Oz again realized that the killing of another child murdering pedophile was still not as satisfying as he thought it would be; even at the wishes of the child from afar. The sick spirit of the pedophile was no longer tied to the pipe with Garret, he had moved on.

Garret was laying there dying, alone and without a mind, spirit or bit of lust to direct him; he was on his own. The thrill of vengeance had eluded Oz. He was beginning to learn that the beast is much bigger and more cunning than he had ever suspected He would need help just to slow it down. He disappointedly headed back to Jason …

Helen suspected something was going on with Jason, but he hadn't told her anything. She loved him and knew him very well. She knew that he had no time for the complications of having other women even though she knew that at times he enjoyed being flirted with and flirting when the opportunity presented itself. When the time came to follow up on his flirting, he turned his head and came home saying "no, thank you."

She loved him most of all because of his compassion for people, especially the underdogs of society. He was very spiritual, sometimes terrifyingly so. He had been known to get angry with God to a point that he would challenge God's desire or his ability to take part in the small lives of the people of these days.

He had no understanding for those that boasted about a day to day relationship with God. But he also lacked the desire to argue with their claim of being all-knowing of God's intentions. He believed in the Golden Rule — do unto others as you would have them do unto you.

Jason was a building contractor and had worked hard most of his 40 years on earth. He loved to debate about race and religion. He almost always won his arguments because he wouldn't get involved unless he knew he was right or that no one could prove him wrong.

He was known to drop a conversation only to go and read up on the topic. He would then bring up the subject when he was better informed.

Lately he'd been bothered by nightmares. Most of them he preferred not to talk about. Often she would be awakened by his subconscious mumbling or his body jerking in the middle of the night. There had been times that she awaken to his sounds and movement and held him tightly until they subsided.

Helen was an excellent mother to her adopted daughter and the two of them spent a lot of time together. She'd moved in with Helen after her marriage to Jason. Sissy had gone through years of child abuse by her parents and constantly had to adjust to her new world of safety and peace of mind. She always referred to Jason has her God-sent angel, even though she had recently learned to call him dad. They were a perfect family of three, with a lot of cruel history behind them.

Jason arrived home about six p.m. after being out all night. He smelled bad and looked like he had not slept for a couple of days.

"Hey, honey, are you all right?"

"No … I haven't been myself lately and I need to talk to you about it when you have time."

"There's no time like now. Sissy won't be home for another hour or so and I'm really starting to worry about you. I mean, I know you're always busy working and providing for us but lately you've been obsessed with a few things that you've said cannot wait.

"You've been spending a lot of time away from home and when I ask if you'd like to talk about it you almost always say 'I don't know what's going on.' That truly doesn't make any sense. I've waited for you to speak with me about it, but we've been missing each other between my obligations and yours. So, talk to me now. I would be more than glad to know what's going on."

Jason sat quietly for a few seconds while Helen waited patiently. "Honey, first of all let me say I love you and that there is no issue about another woman or a business problem that I can't handle. What I'm going through is something that you and I both have encountered when we rescued Sissy from her sexually abusive parents a couple years ago. Do you remember how she used to refer to me as her guardian angel Oz?"

"Boy do I remember. It took us nearly a year to convince her that you weren't him. The psychiatrist was puzzled by it, but if you remember he said it would go away with time and it seems to now be a thing of the past. But what does that have to do with this?"

"Well, most of my nightmares have involved someone named Oz. The weird thing is when Oz is present I'm not a part of my own dreams. Instead of being myself, I'm Oz. I end up with a lot of pieces missing during the times I think I'm asleep. I think I"m actually someplace else, but I can't recall. Yet I'm sure that I was actually where my dreams take me as Oz. I know it doesn't make any sense but today I was somewhere near some railroad tracks having a conversation with a man that I've never seen before. The next thing I know I'm on a bus coming home.

"Now you tell me why didn't I drive my truck or have you take me? The scary part is, I don't remember leaving home or what I actually did while I was gone. All I know is that I'm back here dirty and stinky and puzzled about when it's going to happen again."

"Do you remember anything? Maybe we can piece together what you do remember and figure out what's going on. I must say … a couple of nights ago when I woke you from what I thought was one of your nightmares, you talked to me strangely yet clearly. You told me that some things you have to do are more meaningful to your life of serving mankind than ever before. In fact, you asked me to have faith in you beyond any faith I've had in anything or anyone. You ended by saying that love will see us through and some teacher or something would be put in his place."

"Did I say teacher or mentor," Jason asked.

"You did say mentor. But, honey, I didn't fully understand. I know you are a good man, far better than any man I've ever known. I've always suspected that you were chosen to be here with us for reasons that should not be questioned. I respect my own premonitions when they're that pronounced in my heart.

"I love you very much and I know you're special, just like Sissy says. I'm suspicious that Oz or an angel of some sort, or maybe even God, has given you a mission. I don't question you because I know how strong you are. These dreams you're having are obviously a vital part of your mission. You can rest assured that I trust you and that God will see you through much more positively than my love."

†

89% of child sex assault cases involve person known to the child, such as a caretaker or family acquaintance.

— Diana Russell Survey, 1978

†

CHAPTER THREE

At about 5:30 p.m. there was a knock on the front door followed by the ringing of the front doorbell. Jason listen as Helen asked, "Who's there?" He couldn't hear the response from whoever rang the bell but he did hear Helen ask.,"How are you? What can I do for you?"

"Oh, hi," came the answer. "You don't know me. My name is Ben and I'm an old friend of Jason's. I thought I'd stop in to talk to him for a minute. Is he available?"

"Come in. He's here but I'll need to see if he is busy. I'm sure he isn't too busy for a friend.

"Thank you."

Helen proceeded to Jason and informed him of his guest. "Honey, there's a police officer at the door who says his name is Ben. He says he'd like to speak to you for a moment if you have the time."

"Ben? Of course I have time to speak to Ben," he said as he joined her and walked back to the foyer.

"Benjamin, long times no see. What in the world have you been up to? It's so good to see you. Let me introduce you to my better half, Helen, this is Ben. We've known each other since we were kids."

"Pleased to meet you," Helen said while extending her hand. Ben repeated the pleasure while tenderly shaking Helen's hand.

The two men embraced in a manly way as Ben answered Jason. "I've been around, as you can see. I'm still with the police department looking for a future retirement date so I can be like you and do my own thing. How about yourself?"

"I'm still building and rehabing homes, trying to make the best of it. Hey, you look good. I can see you're still lifting weights. Are you still pressing 500 pounds just for the hell of it?"

"Yeah," Ben answered while rolling his eyes a little and flexing his upper body in a show-off manner for Helen to see.

"I'm pump'n a little bit."

"Come on in and have a seat. Would you like something to drink or eat?"

"No, I came by to talk to you about something that's going on down at the station. It may involve you. I've taken it upon myself to enquire."

"Oh, so this is an official visit?" Jason said while smiling slightly.

"Not really, I just want to give you a heads-up on a concern that I think you should be aware of."

"Do you want me to vacate while you two boys play marbles?" Helen asked jestingly.

"Thank you, that would be nice because we'll probably do some cussing to get some of our boyhood points across," Ben said, also in joking.

As Helen left the living room area, the two men sat down still wearing the semi-smiling faces they'ad started with.

"So what's up, Benjamin?"

"Hey listen, don't let what I'm about to say leave this room. It's kind of official slash unofficial and personal. I know you've read about the guy that sexually molested his own two-year-old daughter over in Braddock."

"Yeah."

"Well … yesterday they found his body. Apparently someone kicked his balls off, tied him with his own shirt and left him down near the wooded area where he had left his daughter to die. They questioned a lot of folks about seeing two men go into the wooded area near Hawkins Village and only one coming out.

"Your name came up because it seems that someone may have used it when they were held in jail overnight on a charge of vagrancy without identification. Whoever this guy is was released once he verified his name and address, which was yours. There was one witness who described the man that came out of the wooded area and he fits your description.

"No one wants to determine how this killer was accidentally released because no one wants the blame. The good part to all of this is that a child murderer is dead. That will save the state thousands of dollars on a trial for a crime that the killer already confessed to then later denied.

"We're not looking at you as a suspect at all. You have an upstanding reputation as a hard working businessman with a couple of heroics under your belt. We all know that you've done your share of protecting women and children. So without being a suspect, you've become a suspect. Do you know what I mean?"

"Yes, I do. And you know something else, I'm glad to hear that he's been dealt with. I wish I could say I did it, but I don't think so."

Ben chuckled a little and asked, "What in the hell does, 'I don't think so' mean? Don't tell me you did it."

"No, I didn't say that I did it," Jason repeated.

"Actually I wish you had. I would be the first to shake your hand. One of the reasons I'd like to retire is that I'm tired of watching pedophiles being slapped on the wrist. The victims are getting younger and younger. There are now more missing children than ever and I suspect that it's because we can't find their bodies. Had that idiot thrown his daughter's body into the storm drain as he said he started to do, this child would have never been found and … he would have undoubtedly killed again."

"Well," Jason responded, "that's an interesting opinion. I've been doing my best to stick with the thought that no one is above the law including men like us. Between you and me, I said I don't think I had anything to do with it because I'm not sure. I certainly don't want to go to jail to prove it by testifying against myself, but I truly have been yearning to do something about it just like you. On top of that, I've been having nightmares for months that seem to indicate names and incidents that have resulted in the deaths of children."

"Wow, that's amazing because so have I. I thought it was because I've read about and pursued so many cases that I'd begun to take them all home."

"What are your nightmares about?" Jason asked.

"It's not just me. Our detective friend Mack down in D.C. is going through the same nightmares. Children come into my dreams asking me to help them take away their pain. I haven't slept very well in months. It just doesn't seem to stop."

"Have they called you by name in your dreams?"

"Actually no, they just refer to me as being "one." One what, I couldn't tell you. Mack says they refer to him as "one" also."

"Have you ever heard the name Oz? I mean have they ever called you Oz?"

Ben paused for a while as if trying to remember every dream to see if he recalled the name OZ. Jason waited patiently.

"The only name that really sticks out in my mind is that of a young girl who always warns me of danger. Her name is Victoria.

She appears on occasion, telling me that my enemy is too big and too cunning. But no, no one named Oz that I can remember."

"Have they ever touched or grabbed you?"

"No, it's just voices and sometimes crying."

"So," Jason said, "what do you think? I mean; what do you intend on doing, if anything?"

"There's nothing I can do, but I do look for the opportunity to do something to save a child. Just today, a four-year-old was murdered by her grandmother's boyfriend who is blaming it on excessive drinking. And I read where they found a missing four-year-old body up in New York, stuffed into his father's duffle bag. It's got to stop. So," he went back to the subject of Oz, "who is this Oz guy that you mentioned? Is he or could he be a suspect?"

"I don't know. In my dreams the children call me Oz. Even my daughter once called me Oz, and I find that kind of scary. Let me just say this … As much as I hate all the violations that are going on seemingly everywhere against young children, I still have a problem playing God, passing judgment and handing out death penalties.

"These people are sick and need help in some cases. After saying all that, in my subconscious there seems to be something telling me that it's about the children, not God. The children are the ones that we need to aid and answer for. They need our help.

"If it were possible, I would gladly stand and give my life to answer just one of their prayers before the predator strikes his final blow. I am, or I believe I am becoming obsessed with this, to the point that my nightmares are encouraging me to go against my better judgment. Does that make any sense whatsoever?" he asked Ben.

"Yeah, of course it makes sense. I'm a sworn officer of the law and I'm not far behind you, except I'd have no problem putting them out of their misery if I could be sure of their guilt."

"Well it seems to be coming from 'the mouths of babes'. They are strangers in my case but a convenient and honest source of witnesses. To bad they're just dreams, huh?"

"Yeah, well we'll see." Ben said as he stood up to leave. "I'll be touching base with you over the next few days. Maybe we can get together and continue this conversation. Oh … and let me know if you talk to Oz. I'd like to give him a hand." "Watch what you say now. From what I understand Oz takes no prisoners." Jason said in a joking way.

"That's my point. I'll cat'cha later Jason. You take care and you know I've got your back." Ben said as he was exiting the front door.

"Tell Helen it's been nice meeting her and I'll be visiting again."

After Ben left Jason went into the next room to talk to Helen. He brought her up to date as to what Ben wanted and went on to tell her about Ben's dream that were similar to his.

"So what do you make of this epidemic against children." Helen asked. "And what do you make of these dreams that now the two of you have been going through?"

"No, there are actually three of us. Ben told me that our friend Mack down in D.C. is suffering with similar dreams. In answer to your question, I really think there's something to it. I know it sound ridiculous but maybe the masses of victims have found a way to be heard," said Jason.

"Yeah or maybe you're just a few good men that are finding these murderers hard to live with and want to do something about it yourselves. Who knows? If I were to guess, I'd say it's the desire to go to their aid that's causing the nightmares."

"You may be right; but remember the children in my dreams are dead already we really can't help them."

"Yeah, but maybe your sorrow for not being able to aid those that are dead is causing you to think of ways to save the living. I don't know. I have no answer about the dreams but I do know that I'm worried that you are hurting much too much about it while you're awake. What's this guy Mack saying about his dreams?"

"Oh, I don't know. I haven't talk to him yet. I plan on calling him later on today."

"I'd imagine that every good man that you talk to about the problem of murdering pedophiles will probably have had some level of nightmares and probably does yearn to help do something to stop it," Helen said.

"Yeah and … I've already told you that my connection with Sissy's Oz is really starting to haunt me even when I know I'm awake."

"Just be careful baby. The subject of children being molested is very touchy for most people. I told you that my cousin Charles down in Florida interfered with a man that was disciplining his five-year-old with a cane. He was arrested and charged with simple assault; then he was jailed and sentence ninety days of incarceration. On a radio talk show about the matter people called in by the dozens with the view that children should definitely be disciplined. You know … it's that old 'spare the rod spoil the child' belief. Ironically the man's child ended up in a near death situation when the man ruptured his son's spleen. Of course that didn't get Chuck out of jail even with the protest of children's rights group on his side."

"Yeah, well next time you talk to chuck ask if he has nightmares about children." Little did he know that he had already met chuck down in Florida and his name was Jax.

"See, you're just joking but I'm being serious. He's a good and innocent man standing up for what is right and he ends up going to jail."

"No, I'm not joking; I truly wonder how deep these nightmares have spread. Ask him the next time you talk to him. I'm actually waiting for my next dream just to see if I can recall a name to check out on the internet and see if they might truly exist. Don't laugh, there maybe something to this."

"I'm not laughing. I just gave you the, 'yeah, right,' because you know that's far fetched.

"Okay," Jason said. "We'll see."

"Okay, let's go to bed so I can put you to sleep right quick before I run out to pick up Sissy from piano class and make a stop at the store," she said with a devilish smile on her face. Jason stood up and gave a fake yawn with a big smile on his face. It was only 7 p.m.

"You ain't sayin' anything that I can't take you up on." They both raced into the bedroom shoving each other and undressing along the way.

It wasn't five minutes after Helen had put Jason to sleep, just as she had said, that Jason went into one of his deep sleep modes. And sure enough, the children began their pleas.

"Mr. Oz, he hurt me terribly. He beat me all over and put me in a bag. I hadn't done anything wrong. I was crying because my tears were hurting inside and mommy won't listen. Mr. Peterson wouldn't stop hitting me after mommy went to work. Please tell him I'm sorry. I didn't deserve to die."

"How old are you, little boy?" Jason asked.

"I'm almost five. I'm too little to punch Mr. Peterson back."

"Where do you live?"

"Mommy said I live at 649 Apple Street. I go to Lincoln pre-school," he said.

"What's your name?"

"Jimmie, my name is Jimmie. Please tell my mommy I'm sorry and that I didn't run away. I just didn't," the child said. "Tell my mommy not to cry because I'm right here. I'm in the bag and I can't get out. I didn't run away," the child repeated.

As the night went on, Jason listened to child after child, just as he had done many nights before. His level of anger reached its peak just short of his deeper unconsciousness. Oz stirred but was unable to maneuver his way into Jason's body.

Oz was listening right along with Jason. He listened and embraced every child with his spiritual blanket of compassion. He struggled but he still could not gain control of Jason's body tonight. Jason was to strongly involved within his own free will. Jason reflected his sorrow and curiosity but refrained from imploding with anger there-by holding Oz with his subliminal restraints.

When Jason woke, he found himself soaking wet with sweat and Helen comfortably lying next to him.

He jumped out of bed and wrote down the names that stood out in his most recent dream and then headed for his computer. Newburgh, New York area ironically had just experience an Amber alert and coincidently the child's name was Jimmie. No one had seen anything suspicious. Four weeks ago the child was reported as missing by its mother and assumed to have been kidnapped. The parents and the community searched high and low with prayers that the child would be returned safely. Jason dreamed that the child was brutally beaten to death and stuffed the duffle bag of his father.

Jason immediately called Ben and told him of his dream and of his research that tied his dream to a reality.

"What's going on Ben? How do you think this could occur? Come on help me out here?" Jason pleaded.

"I don't know, Ben responded in quite a very serious tone of voice. "But I know this — I had a very similar dream two nights ago. It never dawned on me that it could have been real. I'm going to look up the case here at the station and see what I can come up with. I'll call you back."

"You are probably right. I think it would be interesting to know if our dreams have any other similarities. My dreams are so realistic that I'm convinced that they must have some kind of meaning."

"I know that very well, Ben. I'm just playing hunches to see if there may be anything to these dreams and possible premonitions. In the meantime keep me informed about the case. I know it sounds strange but tell the detective up in New York to ask the father where his duffle bag is and see how he responds. I have a feeling that this is not a kidnapping."

"Remember I'm the detective here but you got it man. I'll hit you back later today," Ben said and hung up the phone.

As soon as Ben hung up Helen's cousin Charles was on the line returning her call. After a few greetings and questions Helen remarked that she was glad that he was released and handed the phone to Jason.

"Hello?" Jason said as he walked out of Helen's ear shot. "How are you, man? I'm sorry to hear about your mishap. It sometimes seems that even doing the right thing is wrong to some folks. Good brave men are most definitely hard to find. The reason I asked Helen to call you is because I'm kind of following the patterns of good men to see what it is that we have in common. Helen has made it known that you are one of the good men. Just think what we could do if we have ten good men, when it comes to coming to the aid of children."

"Yeah," he added, "we would all end up in jail."

"Your point is well taken. There's something else I'd like to ask you. This will really sound silly to you. Have you recently had any reoccurring dreams?"

"As a matter of fact I have," Charles answered. "I've been dreaming about helpless children. I think it's because of my incarceration" he paused for a moment and continued. "You know, on second thought that's not true. I was having those same dreams for about a year."

"What are the dreams about?"

"Well mostly about crying children. They often keep me up all night. But they're not ordinary children. They're not crying for toys or stomach aches. They're more or less saying help me and pointing at story like visions that fit into my dreams."

"Have they ever touched you in any way?"

"Only my emotions, sometimes I don't want to wake up and have to leave them behind. Right before I awaken they all try and grab to hold on to me but I'm always beyond their reach."

"Do any of them have names?"

"Oh yes," he answered with excitement. "Victoria, she always warns me not to listen. She always says things like, 'Vengeance is the Lord's.'"

"How old does she appear to be?"

"About ten, I'd guess, but she speaks like an adult at times. She's in nearly every dream. Most of the others speak with their eyes filled with tears, others are just crying out but Victoria seems to change from time to time"

Jason seemed to be on to something but he still was not sure what. He had spoken to two men that he now respected beyond a doubt and one that his wife had praised as a very good man and all three were experiencing similar dreams of crying children. Just for the hell of it he decided to call a man that he knows that sat on the city council.

"Steven?"

"Yeah."

"It's Jason. Hey, look I have a silly question for you. What have your dreams been about lately?"

"That's easy; women and whiskey, sometimes money. Why do you ask?"

"No reason, so how have you been?"

"What do you think about the new proposal to charge taxes on soda pop?"

"That's great, Steven," Jason said as he cut the conversation by saying he'd talk to him later.

He sat back in his chair and doodled on the piece of paper lying in front of him.

He made a few more calls to several men in different fields. The answers were all about deferent things without meaning, some had no dreams at all. It became apparent that; He, Ben, Mack and Charles were special. What ever was happening in Jason's dreams were happening to an elite group of men that were destined to connect. Jason wondered how many more would turn up and how long would it be. Oz was listening … it seemed to him that help may be on its way. It was a long night for Jason. After all of the talk about dreams, he found himself sleepless. At 2:00 a.m. he nudged Helen and began talking.

"I'm puzzled," he said. "All of my life I've questioned the purpose of religion I've made fun of people believing in ghost. People that talk to the dead and beyond have always been a joke to me. Then you have those that speak of super natural or unexplainable phenomena that I've thought as some folk trying to be mysterious for the attention that the unproven occurrence can bring. Now, here I am knowing that men have conjured up all kinds of reasons and excuses as to why they've done their evil things that come directly from their own heart and no place else.

"There are wars going on with a few hundred deaths a year. There are heroic policeman dying in the line of duty to the tone of a couple hundred a year and we give them their due acknowledgement of heroism. Certain groups of people are killed for many different reasons by many different types of murderers. Some become famous killers when the number reaches a number worth reading about in the press. Literally thousands of young men are killed monthly on the street of America; no one cares. Thousand of children are abused, missing or killed each week; no one cares. Public awareness is growing but not nearly fast enough. In some communities missing children reports don't even make the news. Then we have, 'at home pedophiles' that molest and sometimes murder their own children and we are made more aware of who won 'American Idol' than we are of the epidemic of child abuse that has been going on right under our noses. The numbers of unsolved missing or murders children are enough to send fear or at least caution into every household and yet we pretend that the problem is not devastating until it reaches some one we love.

"I wish I could do something to turn pedophilia into a crime without forgiveness in homes and courts across America and maybe even heavens above. I wish it was like a poison fruit you eat it, you die. You molest a child you die. Instead families have been known to make it a best kept secret out of fear of imprisonment. Men have been able to instill enough fear in women and children that they learn to justify the crime by making it the fault of the child or alcohol and drugs.

"I'm so troubled by it that I don't know what to do. And now I'm being haunted with nightmares involving hundreds of children asking me to do something about it. On top of it all I'm not alone in the haunting. Ben, Mack and your cousin are being placed in the same position. Something strange is about to happen. I can feel it coming. Do you know what I mean, honey?" There was no answer. Helen never heard a word. She was sound asleep. She wasn't awakened to the horror. Jason did not speak loud enough. Could he speak loud enough to those outside of his door about the stories that the children are telling him each night? Would he sound crazy if he repeated what he was hearing? Would he be irresponsible if he listens only as a dreamer? Is there a message that he should personally bring awareness to and say to the world I dreamed these truths and they are real? He's only one man not ten or ten thousand. He can only wait for God to direct him.

Jason went to sleep and Oz awakened.

Ten days went by with Jason sleeping through each night without even an inkling of a dream. On the tenth night at 1:30 a.m. Jason's phone rang. It was Ben.

"Jason I need to talk to you. Can you meet me at the walking trail of Frick Park?"

"What's up, man? Are you all right?"

"No, I don't know how I got here and I've been on the verge of passing out. I think I've come here in my sleep and Jason … I think I've come here looking for someone but I can't remember who."

"Where exactly are you?"

"I started at the top of the trail about an hour ago and I don't remember walking down here, but now I'm all the way down by the creek. I'm actually sitting on a stone near the parkway overpass. Oh, one more thing, I think I'm waiting for someone."

"Who?"

"I don't know, my mind has been coming and going. I don't seem to be able to leave. I need you man just come and get me."

"I'm getting dressed as we speak. I'll be there in fifteen minutes. Stay right where you are," Jason said as he bent over to tie his shoes. After driving like a bat out of hell Jason pulled into the upper parking lot of Frick Park. He noticed that there were no other cars. He grabbed his flashlight and ran as fast as he could down the asphalt path that cut into the woods. He was running with the light of the flashlight dancing around and shining in front of him leading the way.

Jason came to a split in the pathway and without hesitation took the gravel covered fork that led to the creek down below. As he got nearer to the bottom he heard a man scream like he had been bitten by a beast. He continued at a slower more cautious pace. He knew he was less than a hundred yards away from the creek when a second scream echoed through the valley. Jason slowed to a walk and quietly used his flashlight to find Ben. He was startled by a pit bull dragging his six foot leash behind him. The dog ran past Jason without looking up or hesitating. Instinctively Jason turned off his light and walked slow enough for his eyes to adjust to the darkness. He could still hear the panting of the pit bull get faint as he continued to follow the path. Now there was not a sound. Jason continued. He was tempted to call out Ben's name but he was unsure of what was going on so he stayed quiet and proceeded.

He began to hear talking. He didn't recognize the voice so he kept cautiously going forward with his light off and nothing in sight. To his left he heard the voice again this time up into the woods and off the beaten path.

Jason's second thought was to now shout Ben's name and simply ask where he was, but no, not Jason, he had a lot of 'I want to be hero in him.' He knew Ben was in some kind of trouble and he wanted to be a part of a rescue. Jason's adrenalin began to pump him up with bravery instead of caution. He stepped up his pace in the direction of the voices. He was suddenly aware of everything around him. The darkness is not as dark when courage sets in. He moved through the brush quickly. Listening, looking and constantly being on guard and ready to act. Jason spotted the figure of a huge man about fifty feet in front of him. He was standing in just enough natural light for

Jason to see that he was looking down and talking boldly to another man lying on the ground. He watched as the night time silhouette delivered a blow down upon the man lying on the ground. Without warning he clicked on the flashlight and shouted like a police officer;

"Don't anybody move!" The light struck Ben in the face first as he stood over the other man that was nearly covered with dirt but still pleading for his life. Jason moved the flashlight back and forth from one to another as he continued to walk toward Ben. Suddenly Ben lit his own flashlight into Jason's face blinding him for a second.

"Oz," he said. "Why are you here?"

"Ben it's me, Jason."

"Why are you here?"

"You called me and asked me to come. What the hell is going on Ben? What's this man doing or what has he done? What the f—k are you doing, man?"

The string of question rolled out as Jason paused not sure of what to do next.

"Oz, he is one. He is a ruthless child killer that has buried his prey for the last time."

Jason was looking directly into Ben's glaring reddish eyes but could not recognize anything of him. His face was bent with anger. His voice was booming, his structure seemed much bigger and taller. His eyes were held wide open and he clenched his teeth between each of his angry words.

"I can't let you do this Ben. You're a police detective not a judge and jury."

Jason was confused but he knew he must stand his ground for what is right.

"Put down the shovel, Ben, and let's get this man to a hospital and then to jail. You can't just bury him alive."

"You mean we can't bury him alive like he did the three young children that he raped and murdered. Is that what you are saying Oz." Ben flashed his light once again up into Jason's face. "You're not Oz." Without another word he gave Jason a tap on the side of his head with the shovel. Jason felt the flat metal shovel smack against his ear. The sound of the contact may have been a thud but for Jason it sounded like metal hitting against a bell. Jason was out like a light. For Jason this night was over as Oz headed home to Helen and went to sleep.

"Honey … honey, why are sleeping out here on the couch?" As she came closer she noticed that the side of his face was swollen. "Oh my God, baby what happen to your face?" Jason was struggling to answer but she didn't give him a chance.

"Are you okay?" she asked as she put her face against his and hugged him in a panic. "Oh baby, let me get some ice and a towel," she said while scurrying toward the kitchen. She continued to ask what had happened without waiting for an answer.

The side of Jason's face was swollen from his chin up to his ear. He sat up trying to get his bearings on just what had happened and to answer his own questions like: How did he get home? What happen with Ben? Who hit him upside his head and a few other things that he couldn't recollect.

His head was still ringing like an ongoing bell and the ringing was crowned with a tremendous headache.

"Here, honey, let's get this ice pack on you and then I'll find you a pain killer. Do you think you need to go to the hospital? I know that's got a hurt. Ah baby, what happened? Were you in an automobile accident? Where's the car? Is it totaled? Where did you go? Ah baby, look at your face it looks like a balloon.

"Wait baby, just slow down a little. I think I'm all right. I just have a terrible headache and I'm still a little fuzzy on what happened. What time is it?"

"It's 7 a.m. Oh, honey, I'm so sorry I didn't even hear you get up this morning.

"Where did you go?" Helen kept firing unanswered questions.

Jason sat still while Helen continued to pamper him and continued to rattle off unanswered questions.

He was doing his best to remember what had happened. He concluded that it must have been a very bad dream.

But how could a dream cause the huge swelling on his face. Everything had happened so fast, just as dreams do. Helen was now mumbling questions while patting and kissing the side of his face.

Jason calmly asked, "Can you please get me a glass of water, baby?"

"Yes; oh yes, I didn't think of that," she said as she headed back to the kitchen.

Jason picked up his cell phone and took a look at his recent calls that had been made and received. Ben, Ben, Ben … all Ben. After a few seconds of thought, he pushed the recall button and called Ben. After four rings Ben answered.

"Hey man, good morning to ya. What's up?" he asked as if there was nothing unusual to talk about.

"Please don't play games with me Ben. You know why I'm calling. What the hell is wrong with you? Why would you hit me?"

"What are you talking about?"

"Come on man don't play, this is serious. There's nothing to joke around about. My head is swollen like a watermelon and I'm not at all happy about it. I want to know what made you hit me and what did you end up doing?"

"Man I don't know what you're talking about. I just got to work and I'm on a very serious case. And while I'm always glad to talk with you, right now there's a child rapist that may be getting away. You must be having one of your dreams and I really don't have the time to chat right now."

"Wait, don't hang up, listen to me, look at your cell phone calls." Jason waited.

"I didn't know you had called Jason. What did you want at that time of morning?"

"Look again, we talked each time you called me and I returned your calls."

"What did we talk about?" Ben began to calm down to look for an explanation.

"Are you telling me that you don't remember talking to me at all?"

"No, I don't."

"Do you remember busting me in the face with a shovel?"

"Look, I admit I don't remember talking to you, but I can definitely tell I haven't been anywhere near you. I got up this morning at 6 a.m. and got here at 6:30 a.m. and that's where I've been until this moment."

Jason realized that Ben didn't have the slightest bit of memory about what happen last night.

"Look, Ben, I've got to digest all of this and check a few things out. I'll call you later on today please answer my call because I think I know what happened," Jason said.

"All right, hit me back," Ben said and hurriedly hung up.

After letting Helen continue to baby him for a while he got up and without a shower or a shave headed back to Frick Park. Down the asphalt walkway onto the gravel path and down toward the creek. He slowed as he approached the bottom of the path. He wasn't exactly sure where he had turned up into the area where Ben had been digging. Then he noticed ruffled leaves and a faint indication that the area had been walked upon. He walked up and over a small mound about fifteen yards. The gravel path behind him was totally out of site. After another five yards or so he knew that he was standing next to a freshly dug grave site that had been covered with leaves. Jason jerked suddenly as his memory recalled the whack that he had gotten last night with the flat end of Ben's shovel. This was clearly the place. He took his foot and kick away leaves and some of the dirt at what had to be the feet or the head of the man that was being buried by Ben. After a few kicks he bent over and pulled some dirt away exposing the shoes still on the feet of a man that was obviously dead.

"Oh, my God," he said out loud. "Ben actually murdered this man." He looked around to see if anyone was in sight that may have seen him come up over the hill. There was no one in sight. Jason kicked the dirt and then more leaves over the bottom of the body and nervously walked back to his car.

"Why?" he kept asking himself. "Why would Ben take a man's life?" A sworn officer of the law had committed the ultimate crime and Jason witnessed at least a part of the killing. On that long walk back Jason pondered what he should do. He also wondered why Ben had called him Oz and why Ben did not seem to respond to his own name or why Ben couldn't recall being in the park even though he knew he must have talked to me according to his cell phone list of calls. Jason became overwhelmed. He pulled over to the curb and turned off his engine. After sitting a few moments he flipped his phone open and called Ben.

"Hello, Detective Ben," he answered.

"Yeah, Ben, it's me, Jason. Do you have a moment to talk?"

"Yeah, it's been a hell of day for us. We had a positive I.D. on a man in Wilkinsburg that raped and buried a six-year-old. We surrounded his home where we knew he was yesterday. We had watched his house all night making sure we wouldn't loose him while we sought a warrant for search and his arrest. Somehow he got away during the night while we had the hours."

"How'd you find her place of death?" Jason asked.

"You know it's funny that you should ask. I was part of the search team that was actually looking in the wrong area and I played a hunch and went right to her body. She had been dead for about eight to ten hours. I had the place under total surveillance. I spent three hours there myself before they informed me that they were going to move in first thing this morning. That's why I didn't have time to really talk to you earlier. I think we will get him. This scum needs to be put to rest. I was there when they found the six-year-old girl's body. In her hand we found the creep's military dog tag. She hung onto the ultimate clue and he never knew it. He just covered her with a mound of dirt where she died. I was angry at myself that I could not find her soon enough to save her life."

"Ben I think I know where he is," Jason said.

"You're kidding me right?"

"No, I think I know where he is," Jason repeated.

"Listen Ben, I've got to talk to you alone first and then you can do what you need to do."

"Wait, Jason this is no game if you know where he is we don't want to let this child killer get away. No child is safe while he's free. We found evidence that he may have murdered as many as four children over the last three years. So don't play way this Jason this is extremely serious."

"Don't worry Ben. This time he can't get away. Believe me on this one."

"Where is he Jason?"

"Meet me at Frick Park; I'm only a half block from there. I'll turn around right now and meet you on the North Braddock Avenue side upper parking lot; the one near the tennis court."

"Okay, I'll be there in ten minutes let me notify the swat team and the county office, I hope you know what your t talking about."

"No Ben, just you. Once we confirm you can do what you need to do, but for now just me and you; Okay?"

"Okay, I'll see you there shortly. Jason if he gets away and I didn't follow procedure I'll lose my job and even worst, like I said he's a dangerous man, some child may lose his or her life."

"Don't worry, he won't get away this time I promise," said Jason.

Ben pulled into the lot less than thirty minutes later. He cautiously looked around as Jason walked up to the car.

"Where is he Jason?"

"I'm almost one hundred percent sure that he is here in the park down near the creek," Jason responded.

"I got to call for back up Jason you're not a police officer and you could get hurt this guy is no joke," Ben said as he opened the car door and stood up.

"Ben he's dead! Do you hear me Ben I said, he's dead! Do you have a shovel?" Jason asked.

"No I don't."

"Is there anything in your trunk we can dig with?"

"I don't know let's look and see." Ben opened the trunk of the unmarked car. The open trunk revealed a shovel that appeared to have been recently used.

"Well I guess I do have a shovel. How in the world did it get into my trunk; I don't know."

"Maybe one of the other detectives had it."

"No I've had this car for at least a week by myself; that's strange."

"Nonetheless, let's go," Jason said.

As they took the quarter mile walk down the trail Ben began to ask questions.

"How'd he die Jason?"

"I don't really know. I just know he's dead."

"How'd you know where his body was or should I ask how'd you find him here?" "I got a tip and followed up in the wee hours of this morning."

"At night Jason, why didn't you call 911?"

"It's a complicated story Ben you'll understand in a minute," he answered.

"I guess I've got to ask you the big question Jason. Did you kill him?"

"I don't think so Bennie," Jason answered.

"Do you know who did?"

"As a matter of fact I think I do."

Ben glanced over at Jason as they both walked without missing a step while tilting his head as if he has figured out a solution or answer to a problem.

When they came to the point of turning off the gravel path up into the woods Jason intentionally slowed down but continued to walk past it to see if Ben would start to recall anything. Ben continued to walk along with Jason.

"Wait I passed the place we were supposed to turn. It's back up in here."

He pointed as he turned around and headed up into the woods with Ben following right behind.

As they approached the mound that covered the body Jason kept glancing at Ben to see his expression. Ben dodged tree branches as he walked but never indicated that he had been here before.

"That's where he's at," Jason said while pointing at the hump of leaves. Jason reached for the shovel that Ben had been carrying.

"No Jason I can't let you touch anything. There may be evidence that will be needed to clear this up." Ben carefully walked up to the body signaling Jason to stay back. He used the shovel to remove some dirt and dead leaves from what appeared to be the back of the man's head. Ben kneeled down and carefully turned the man's face toward him.

"That's him," Ben stated. "It looks like someone bashed him in the back of his head." Ben stood back up and faced Jason. "I'm going to have to arrest you Jason. Your story makes no sense. And as much as I wanted to see this man die you can't kill. The laws must be upheld. He had a right to a trial. And though I love you like a brother and I know he's guilty, you didn't have the right to take his life. You could have very well murdered an innocent man. I've got to take you in man."

"I know you do but listen to me Ben. I didn't do it. I couldn't help but notice that when you got out of your car there was mud all over the driver's side floor. And, the shovel that you took from the trunk was covered with the same reddish mud right here on the ground. How do you think you knew which end was his head when the mound is rounded on both ends. And, I can show you something else. Before I left here earlier to call and bring you here I knocked away a few leaves and I noticed that the man is cuffed with his arms behind his back," Jason said while knocking away the same leaves that he had put back earlier. "And look what we have … cuffs with your name inscribed on them. Where are your cuffs Ben? I noticed when you were getting out of the car that your cuff holster was empty. And, here's the kicker Ben, I was here last night when you knocked him out and buried him alive. And, you are the one that slapped me with that very same shovel that you're holding. No Ben I didn't do it; you did."

Ben stood directly in front of Jason with a very puzzled look on his face.

"What in the f — k are you talking about?" he asked as he bent over to examine the cuffs. "Oh my f—king God! How could this be? I've never been here in my life."

"Ben listen to me, you were here last night. I'm proud of you. But just like you said earlier we can't be judge and executioner. I don't know what to do. There's a lot at stake here. If we call the coroner's office they'll know in no time that you or I had something to do with it. You make the call."

"The call is I'm getting my cuffs. We'll cover up this piece of shit as you call him and get out of here. No one will find him here and soon the summer under brush will cover this whole area with vines and thorns."

Ben had bent over to unlock his cuffs, while Jason started to dig dirt and leaves back onto the corpse.

While Ben was bent down Jason followed his notion to slap Ben on his muscular back as hard as he could.

"What the f — k are you doing."

"That's for getting us into this shit and for you hitting me on the side of my head and knocking me out. You should be glad I didn't go up side your head. I just didn't want to have to drag your big ass back to the car. Let's get out of here," Jason said as they both hustled away while looking around to see if anyone was in the area.

Two uneventful weeks went by for Jason. He had an occasional call from Ben letting him know that he hadn't heard anything pertaining to the Frick Park incident and that he had been sleeping well and free of any memorable dreams. They both knew it wouldn't last. Something was brewing they just couldn't begin to imagine what.

＊ ＊ ＊ ＊ ＊

Thursday, April 4 at 6:50 a.m. Jason received a call from Ben.

"Mack's been suspended from duty down in D.C."

"Why? What happen?"

"He said he was accused of using excessive force in the apprehension of, guess what … a pedophile."

"Why doesn't that surprise me?"

"You know Mack is not the type to step over any limits. He's about as straight as a man can be. The man is in a coma from what they're saying was blunt force trauma that occurred when Mack was trying to make the arrest when the suspect ran with only Mack in pursuit. By the time the rest of the officers caught up to the chase the suspect was lying at Mack's feet with a broken neck and concussion. They said it doesn't look like he'll recovery from the injuries," Mack said when he caught up to the suspect he was already down and unconscious. But a witness said she seen Mack catch up with the man and ram his head first into a concrete wall after talking to him for a few minutes. Mack told me he remembered chasing the man but he doesn't remember catching up to him. He said he recalls standing over the man when the other officers approached. He watched them lift him up to secure him. They were scuffling with him a little while trying to cuff him just before he collapse to the ground. Once he was lying on the ground Mack said it was as though someone turned the sound back on. He was suddenly aware of what was going on and instructed someone to call the paramedics. He said he doesn't remember touching the man at all."

"Well I certainly believe him. Don't you? What do you want to do?"

"Let's go down to D.C. and see what we can do. At least we can talk to Mack and let him know he's got support," Ben said.

The two men packed up and headed for Washington which is about a four and a half hour drive from Pittsburgh. They had stopped for gas at Breezewood, Pa. when Jason got a call from Charles down in Jacksonville.

"Hello?" Jason answered and was nodding his head while Ben looked on thinking it may have been something about Mack.

"Are you sure it wasn't just a dream?" Jason asked. He listened for nearly ten minutes before speaking. "I see; listen, don't do anything or say anything to anyone. I'm on my way to Washington, D.C. with Ben. I will call you in a little bit. Remember don't do anything but rest until I talk to you again. Repeat that name to me. I'm going to see if I can find out who he is. All right, I'll call you later," Jason said and hung up the phone. Ben was eagerly waiting for Jason to tell him what had caused his facial expression to go from concern to fear.

"What's up?" Ben asked as he started up the car.

"Well it seems that our excitement has no end. Charles down in Florida believes that he may have killed a man two nights ago. He said he watched this evening news that was reporting the discovery of a man's body just off a highway not far from where he lives. He noticed when the officials where carrying the body up the hill side that it was wrapped in an Indian blanket. He said he recognized that he had one just like it and went to see if his was still on the back seat of his car where he used it to cover his torn seat. He said it wasn't there. Oh yeah, he also said when awakened that morning he was covered with mud. A final piece of news; the police was looking for the dead man for more than a week. He had been seen snatching a young child out of a Wal-Mart Store and was the center of an Amber Alert."

"This isn't good," Ben said.

"I know, I'm just wondering if it's going to get worse," Jason said.

"How are you going to handle that one?" Ben asked.

"I don't know, but one thing for sure, these things that are happening aren't random occurrences. We are on a mission rather we want to be or not," Jason said.

"Well we've got to stop. We can't justify these acts under any circumstances."

"So what do you think we should do?"

"I personally think we should get together as soon as we all can; You, Mack, Charles and I. We need to figure out what's going on within us that's causing us to take the law into our own hands. I don't know about you but I'm definitely getting worried about what I'm capable of doing. I'm even more worried about what you are capable of doing after what we've experienced."

"Let's get to Mack first and see exactly what happen and maybe the Florida thing is just a coincident," Ben said.

Jason nodded and said, "I hope your right. I'm going to call Charles and see if he can get a flight out to Washington tonight. It may be time for us to compare dreams a littler closer. My daughter lives in Largo; we can meet at her place and see if we can some how change our own destiny."

Jason confirmed a flight for Charles that would arrive at 10:00 a.m. the morning of the next day. Ben called Mack and informed him of tomorrow's meeting between the four of them. He told Mack that he would explain when he gets there. He told him to stay secluded and advised that he shouldn't talk to anyone until he had been brought up to date about a couple of unexplained occurrences. Mack reflected that it would not be a problem and for Ben to just call and he would be ready.

During their last two hours of the drive to Washington, Jason and Ben compared a lot of thoughts and opinions about their feelings and most certainly their compassions for the safety of women and children against rape and abuse.

Ben and Jason both had relatives in the Washington, D.C. area, so they parted and agreed to meet in Largo at 1:00 p.m. the following day.

†

The typical offender is male, begins molesting at age 15, engages in a variety of deviate behavior, and molests an average of 117 young-sters, most of whom do not report the offence.

— Dr. Gene Abel in a National Institute of Mental Health Study

†

75% of the violent victimized children took place in either the victim's home or the offender's home.

— BJS Survey of State Prison Inmates

†

"When someone enacts an urge or desire to violate a child in a sexual or abusive way that person should face our capital punishment and nothing less"

— Ahmad Hakeem,
Collage student of engineering

CHAPTER FOUR

After formally introducing those that had never met, Jason took the lead and got right down to the concerns that had brought the four men together.

"Ben and I have discovered that the four of us have more in common than we think. We're starting to believe that we are being driven by our dreams to a point that we are acting out in violent ways while we are asleep. I guess it's kind a like sleep walking. The only difference is that we are physically encountering people that are real. That's not the worse part. It is possible that we've taken the lives of men that our subconscious believes needs to be destroyed; mainly child molesters and child murders. This morning Ben talked to the lady that witnessed Mack's attempt to apprehend the pedophile murderer. Once she was informed that the suspect was the child murderer that every law official in the area was looking for she retracted her story that she had made by phone to the local police about seeing Mack kill the man. However, early this morning Ben convinced her that we were on the defense for our friend and she showed us something that she hadn't shown to anyone else. She had recorded everything that happened that night on her cell phone video recorder. Ben had it down loaded and I brought it here for us to view together. No one else in this room has seen what's on the CD other than Ben, the lady and I. After we view it here I plan on destroying it for good."

Jason loaded the photo software into the computer and hit the play button.

"As you can see she started her camera phone as the suspect ran and trapped himself at a closed entry to the subway just below her window.

It's not that clear but you can see Mack slowly walked up on the suspect with his gun drawn. He appears to be telling the man to put his hands behinds his head and to get down on his knees; as you can see, the suspect is obeying Mack's commands. Now Mack, as you see, is walking around the man and appears to be having a conversation with him. At first the suspect is shaking his head no and then right here, he starts to laugh while still down on his knees. Both Mack and the suspect at this point are looking around to see where the additional officers were. Now watch this; Mack pauses behind the man while the suspect begins to laugh again. Mack grabbed him by the back of his shirt and lifted him off the ground with one hand. Then he began to ram the man's head against the concrete barrier; once, twice and then a third time as the man went limp and fell to the ground. This becomes a little bazaar as Mack seems to be talking to him while he lies unconscious upon his face and non-responsive. Now watch what happens. Mack appears to look up at the lady doing the recording. I'm going to stop it right there and zoom in as closely as I can without losing focus. Now look, right there, look at the color of Mack's eyes."

"Wow they are almost bright red"

"That's correct, his eyes seem to be ferocious and we know Mack is not a ferocious man. After thirty years on the police department they say he has never even pulled out his weapon on anyone. Now he looks off up the side walk and then he quickly collapse into the corner and seemingly exhausted and losing consciousness. And then within seconds he stands upright and draws his weapon as if he just spotted the suspect lying on the ground at his feet. And then of course the other officers ran up and appear in the footage grabbing up the suspect and roughing him a little and putting cuffs on him. But as you can see the man is nothing but a limp body as they lifted him off the ground. And if you look closely right here you can see that as incoherent as he is he is smiling as if he has found pleasure even in his rough and tumble capture."

Mack had watch quietly like the others. He was shaking his head all the while.

"Wow, I don't recall any of that. If I wasn't looking at this I would swear to you that it couldn't have possibly been me. And yet there I am as clear as day. I don't even remember going to assist in the apprehension in the first place. Yet there I am. I don't know what to make of it. There's just nothing I can say. I'm guilty as sin without an inkling of memory," Mack said.

"You're not alone," Ben said. "We're all in the same boat. I need to hear from Charles before I can elaborate on what our police records have indicated over the last eight month. It will both shock you and satisfy you as a good and protective man. So let's get to it. What happen to you Charles?"

"I wish I had a story to tell. I can't recall anything that I've done after going to sleep," Charles said and continued. "I know by some of my morning afters that two or three of what I thought were good nights of sleep, I've awaken like a man that has just returned from a battle in an alleyway. The worse evidence against myself is that three out of the last four bodies that have turned up in Jacksonville are men that where at one time or another convicted of child molestations and worse. This last victim, as I told Jason, had been on the news for three days as a suspected child adductor and they haven't found the child but they did find his body off of Highway 95 yesterday. You know the rest of that story."

"I told Ben and Mack in different conversations that you recognized that the blanket that the man's body was rapped in, may have been yours, well … not may have been but was yours for sure," said Jason.

"Not only that, I've have been following the news stories of both wanted child killers, now three, these suspected child molesters have been very strong suspects in each news story. Some how I know that I have hunted them down and that I have done the unthinkable. I really need to know what to do. And you know I have an arrest record after that event with the man that was beating his own child with a stick and I intervened to stop it. If I am a one man Jacksonville vigilante it's not because I'm trying to be it's that I can't help being," Charles said.

Ben looked over at Jason and nodded his head yes. Ben brought out some statistics that he had followed up on involving killings of known pedophiles in each of the cities that the four men lived in.

"Here are the facts in the Pittsburgh area. There have been more than thirteen known pedophiles found dead or have been reported missing in the last eight months. In the Washington, D.C. area there have been twelve that they know of. In the Jacksonville area there has been fifteen. Baltimore has had twenty-two; which indicates there are more of us. There have even been outbreaks like ours in Cleveland and the small city of Johnstown, Pennsylvania. I don't think me or Jason has made it that far.

"I beg to differ with you. I believe I've gone further than that. I've check my own business schedule from last year. Every city that I've done business in, or visited while alone, has had at least one murder on the date that I was there. So needless to say Charles I've become much more dangerous than you. I'm saying that I think I actually committed the crimes, but I believe that some how I'm being or have been spiritually hypnotized into being a part of these killings. The police don't search hard for the killers of child rapist and murders but sooner or later these statistics are going to become apparent and the higher authorities will have to do their jobs. As much as I've always wanted do something about the abuse and murder of children I never dreamed I'd really do anything like this. Ironically

'Dreamed" is the key word for all of us. Here's what we know, number one; all of us have been lead by our dreams to the pedophiles. Number two; the children of our dreams seem to be trapped in our subconscious. Once their predator has deceased they in turn are released. The voices of my children are very protective of children that have yet to become victims. They seem to want the threat of other children eliminate also. Number three; none of us can remember any of our activities once we are asleep. Even though Ben called me in the middle of his, let's just call it 'task' on one occasion. Yet, we all remember one particular child named Victoria that seems to be warning us instead of telling us her story.

Number four; I believe we all take on much stronger body strength when we go out into the night and obviously our eye color changes to a burnt orange or red as we seen with Mack. That may be due to adrenalin or the justifiable motives making us that furious. Number five; we all have a daytime reputation of being responsible gentlemen that would give up their shirt to help someone else. Number six; there seems to be some form of conduit between us. We seem to be connected to each in some small way. Why, is a mystery, because none of us are blood relative and none of us want to kill. Finally, another thing that's for sure; by the number of pedophiles turning up dead there must be more of us. On the night that Ben had his encounter he told me that the man was one of them. I don't know what that means. It could be that there is a list of them that we all know of or that we each have a list of our own. Ben also called me Oz, which is ironically the name that the children of my dreams call me. No one else has been called Oz, so I'm guessing Oz may be the center of my rebellion and that eventually he will appear in all of your dreams too, especially since Ben is aware of him," Charles interrupted Jason.

"I guess I didn't tell you, my dream children sometime call me Jax … I thought they were talking to another person until they made sure that I knew it was me. One of them actually wrote the name Jax on my wall, but when I woke up it was gone"

"Has anyone else heard the name Jax in their dreams?"

"No" was both of their answers.

"So, here we are with a big question of what do we do next while we are awake?"

Ben responded, "I think we should gather every piece of information that we can about missing children in each of our regions and compare them to each of our dreams. Any names that the children give us we should write down as soon as we can. Time, places and names, let's get them, research them and see if we can make sense of our dream missions before they get us killed or arrested for murder. In the mean time I think we should hand cuff ourselves at night to our beds or something near by."

"I think I'll cuff myself to my woman," Mack said and got a burst of laughter.

"That is a good idea," Charles said. "Then she can't go wondering off to some other bedroom." Then there was more laughter.

"Laughter is good," Jason said and continued. "I get the feeling that we won't have a lot to laugh about until we're done doing what ever it is we're being brought together to do."

Ben continued "After we get all of our facts and compare notes we'll come back together and work as a team to get this shit out of our minds."

"Amen to that," Mack said.

"Listen," said Jason. "Let's give it two weeks. The days will be longer and we can all take off from our jobs and maybe convince our women that this is something we can't live through if we don't get to the bottom of these dreams that are turning to living nightmares. I, for one am ready to do whatever it will take to end the nightmares and I'll do what I can to help stop the rape and murder of children. If that means killing, then so be it. But, I'd much rather see our judicial system wake up and approach this disease at its roots."

"I haven't said much," said Charles. "But I've probably have already done too much against the foes of these babies. I feel a lot like you Oz, if they rape and kill our babies there'll be no trial. Forgive me if I'm sounding forwardly aggressive; but after hundreds upon hundreds of so called missing children that turn up murdered at the hands of child pedophiles we have no choice but to stand up. I personally have no mercy."

"I guess you know that you just called me Oz," Jason said.

"Yeah, I heard that to," said Ben. "But in that line of conversation Oz fits the script a hell-of-a lot better than you Jason or me or any of us. I'm in agreement with Charles; it's time to act instead of praying for resolve. Once we are informed with the facts without any room for doubt, I too believe that I'm capable of striking while am awake. I won't have to go to sleep to do what should be done by all men. That is to protect our women and children. Killing is sometimes a necessary evil especially when it's in reaction to evil perpetrated against babies.

We're like soldiers now; when a soldier goes to war he's neither judge nor jury nor is he an arresting officer. The gavel has been swung; molest a child; meet your maker. That's my thought while I'm wide eyed and awake." Ben quickly tilted his head and rolled his eyes for all to see that he meant business. He nearly growled before asking Mack of his opinion.

"Well …" Then after a long pause he continued. "We can't take the law into our own hands as we've all hinted time and time again, but listen, I have the feeling that these killers have been judged and convicted by not only the children that haunt us but by God Himself. There have been many bible verses saying that the voice of God has been sent by many messengers to destroy one false idol or another. These men believe they are as gods; that they can take for themselves and suffer no consequences until judgment day. I think, may God forgive me if I am wrong, we should do God's will."

'I'll, Amen that one myself," said Jason. "So here's to our willingness to sacrifice all that we hold as sacred and dear to ourselves for the sake of children of any race, creed or color. In belief that we shall help remove this disease and many lives will be spared in the name of God. And to those who believe that their overwhelming lust for babies has no cure; we object with faith and commitment that we are a part of that cure. Your life as you know it may be taken as such 'as you have killed you shall also die'. If we should kill for the sake of what is right we too shall perhaps die for the sake of righteousness. I guess I can get an Amen too … well … please fellas.

"Amen" said three men with one voice.

Jason spent most of his days in anticipation of the battle that he and his comrades were about to embark upon. Oz took advantage of every moment that he could to utilize Jason's flesh to pursue his quest for revenge.

∗ ∗ ∗ ∗ ∗

Thursday May 1ˢᵗ 12am:

Jason was awakened by the crying of a six-year-old girl. He glanced down over his own feet where she was standing the foot of the bed. He recognized the stress and severity of this little girl's pain. She was soaking wet from head to toe. She had long blond hair and eye shadow mixed with her tears running down her face. Her lips were painted red but washed off and dirty on more than half of her bottom lip. She wore a shoe string blouse of which one strap was torn off and hanging while the other barely held up over her shoulder. Her tears were visible through all of the makeup and moisture on her cheeks. She wore no under garments or any clothes at all below her waist. In her hand she had one small high heeled black shoe. Blood appeared to slightly mix with water and running down her legs. She stood still leaning against the far wall where there were typically eight or ten children during some of Jason's nightmares. She hadn't uttered a word. Jason jumped up and got down on his knees in front of her.

"Child" he said "What has happened to you?" impulsively he picked her up and stood up with her hugged against his chest. "Poor baby … you poor child." He turned and looked at Helen who was as usual sound a sleep. Jason attempted to walk back along the side of the bed and seek Helen's help but found that he was unable to enter that space. His legs would not allow him to walk past the beds foot board. He drew his attention to the phone and decided to call 911 but again he could not enter that part of the room with the child in his arms.

"What has happened? Who has done this to you?"

"My daddy … my daddy hurt me and threw me into a hole in the ground filled with water. My daddy is bad, he hates me," she said.

"Nobody could hate you. What's your name?"

"Susan Reed, I'm almost six years old. I'm a model for my daddy when mommies away. My daddy makes me pretty. He told mommy I ran off into the trees but I didn't. He hurt me and took me there."

"You precious child you'll be all right now. I've got you and I'm not going to let anyone hurt you. Where are you hurt? Jason asked, forgetting that this must be a dream.

"Right here," she said while touching or signifying her heart. Jason attempted to open the bed room door but he couldn't get close enough to touch the knob. "Don't let my daddy hurt my little sister please. She's only four and she models too." Jason remembered what Ben had said about gathering information.

"Where do you live?" he asked.

"I live in Youngstown."

"What's your mommy and daddy's name?"

"Sarah," she answered. "Mommy's name is Sarah; my daddy's name is David."

Jason placed her down onto the floor and attempted again to open the door. This time it opened, but when he step out of the room and looked back into the room it was too dark to see the child. Jason reached around and clicked on the bed room ceiling light and exposed only Helen curled up and still fast asleep. He shook his head after realizing all this was just another of his realistic dreams. He went into the bathroom and put his face just a few inches away from the mirror. He felt relieved on one hand and confused on the other for a brief moment he thought he heard someone call the name Oz. He reared back a little and covered his face with both hands.

"What am I going to do?" He said to himself. After slightly shaking his head no, he turned off the bathroom light and opened the door that lead into the hall. Before he could enter back into his bedroom he stumbled into two small black children that were standing in the short hallway. He reached back and turned the bathroom light on exposing the two faces peering up at him. They too were soaked from head to toe and clothes down to their waist. They both wore plats with barrettes clipped at the base of each of their hair. One of the little girls appeared much paler than the other and her face and skin seemed to droop as if she were beginning to rot. Again Jason found himself on his knees this time embracing these two young girls that he estimated were about five years of age. They both spoke first in unison and then separately.

"Mr. Earl put me in a big can," they said together.

"What are your names?" Jason asked.

"Anita."

"Christie," said the other.

"What is your last name, Anita what?" Jason asked.

"Clark, Anita Clark," she said in her very childish sounding voice.

"Where do you live?"

Anita hunched her shoulders as Christie answered. "Bonifay St. Pittsburgh."

"How old are you?"

"Five," they both said.

Anita seemed older than the other girl, and said, "I've been in the metal can much longer than Christie. Mr. Earl put her in to play with me. But we can't play in the can. We can only make wishes together. We wished that you could hear us, so that you can take us out of the can."

"Where is the can?" Jason asked.

"Bonifay Street near where we lived. Sometimes we hear people outside but they can't hear us. Until you, we could only speak to each other."

"What's Mr. Earl's last name?"

"I don't know," Anita answered as she hunched her shoulders.

Again Christie answered. "Norton, he's my mommy's boyfriend. She sometimes calls me Christie Norton."

"Is he your daddy?" Jason asked

"No," she answered. "He's just my mommy's boyfriend, my daddy's name is daddy," she said with pride.

"What's your mommy's name?"

"Mommy," Anita answered. "Rita Clark, I mean Rita Clark is my mommy's name."

"My mommy's name is Marie," said Christie.

"How long have you been in the can?" Jason asked both of them.

"I don't know for sure. I was there a long time before Christie came."

"I don't know," Christie said.

"What does the can look like?" asked Jason.

"It's big and round with screws coming into it and it's always been filled with water. Can you get us out Mister Oz? Please? We want to play like other kids. Can you tell my mommy where I'm at?" Christie asked.

Jason stood up right closed his eyes and leaned against the outside of his bedroom door for a few moments while both girls watched him.

"Mister Oz we're tired, too."

"Yes and we didn't do anything wrong so why did Mr. Norton put us here?"

"I don't know but I will find you and get you out. I promise you that!"

The door suddenly opened behind him and the light from outdoors was shining into the room through the patio door.

"Good morning honey who were you talking to," asked Helen.

"Oh … I think I was talking to Anita and Christie".

"Oh yeah, right … and where are they?"

"You know how my dreams are. They're so real that I don't know whether I'm asleep and dreaming or awake inside of my dream," Jason answered.

"Well I've got to wake up Sissy for school and I'm on an all day quest for information about our income for the tax accountant. How about you? What does your day look like?" Helen asked.

"Well I too am on a quest for information but it's really not worth talking about at this point. I'll bring you up to date later. Oh, and I may be gone for a couple of days. I'm going to help Ben follow up on a very important matter up in Youngstown"

"I hate when you leave us for these trips. I worry and I miss you so much. When do you think this will all end and you can spend more time with us?"

"Soon; I promise you that it won't be long. I love you very much and in order for my love to mean anything I've got to fulfill this commitment. Please have patience with me. I'll be safe and I'll make it up to you and Sissy."

"You're a strong man Jason. I've got just as much faith in you as I do God. I know you're on a mission and I know you'll do what's right; I also know that nothing will stand in your way. Something is calling into our lives, so...get it done honey, just be careful. Sometimes having God on your side is not enough." Helen stood up on her toes and kissed him on the lips "You seem to be getting taller or maybe I'm getting shorter. Oh well, it doesn't matter, we're the same height when we're lying together" she said with a smile and a wink.

Jason couldn't wait to get the information about his dream to Ben to be checked out. With a quick call ahead he headed down to Bens office. By the time he arrived Ben had pulled as much in formation on the names, places and where- bouts on the three children. . When he walked into Ben's office he knew something was brewing just by the expression on Ben's face.

"Listen, those two folders contain information about the names you gave me. All three are real life missing children. Even the names you gave me in association with them are coincidently real. You go ahead and look through them and see what you come up with. I've got to go out on a case and hopefully make an arrest. I'll be back as soon as I can, and you can then bring me up to date."

Jason read through the folders of the three missing children. One in Youngstown Ohio named Susan Ella Reed age 5, missing since November 2009, mothers name Sarah Reed, fathers' name Jeffrey Reed, believed to be abducted by a missing local man named Roger Moore; a second right here in Pittsburgh named Anita Ann Clark age 5, missing from Bonifay Street St. Clair Village a public housing complex on the South Side Heights, mother Rita Rae Clark and fathers name unknown, reported missing by her mother on December 3rd 1980, last seen asleep at 210 Bonifay Street 10 p.m., suspiciously abducted from opened rear window; a third child 5 years old Christina Williams, mothers name Marie Williams Norton, fathers name David Roscoe of Washington DC., at home step father name, Earl Watson Norton, last seen at home 214 Bonifay St. date reported missing, April 2nd 1986, reported to have walked away from home while Mr. Norton babysat. Mother was reportedly out at local bar, discovered child missing at 2:30 am upon returning home. Mr. Norton had apparently drank himself to sleep at about 11p.m. the night before the child was reported missing; suspicion that the child may have walked out to find her mother between 11 p.m. and 2:30 a.m.

Jason decided to take a ride up to St Clair Village which had long been an abandoned. He drove on Fisher St. until he came upon what was Bonifay St.; Jason turned left and drove slowly looking for the addresses 210 and 214. He came to 214 first and parked his car and began to look around the building for anything that resembled a round can with screws in it that could hold two children. After searching outside and inside from basement to the third floor of the empty building he moved onto building 212 and again found nothing. Lastly he entered into building number 210 the doors were missing and all of the windows had been knocked out. He started on the top floor and worked his way down to the basement boiler room. He found nothing. As he exited the building his phone rang, it was Ben.

"Are you still there? I'm headed back to the office now. I should get there in twenty minutes or so. Did you find anything relevant to your dreams in the folders?"

"Well, as you know the names did match. I took a ride up here to old St. Clair Village and walked through three of the buildings, but, there's nothing that even resembles any kind of metal can with screws sticking in to it."

"Well, those buildings have been abandoned for years. In fact I read where they are schedules to be torn down this year. I'd imagine anything metal would have been taken for scrap," Ben stated.

"Yeah", Jason responded, "the only metal left in these buildings are the huge boiler tanks. There too big to be taken, you'd need a crane," Jason said.

"Yeah I guess they'll just bulldoze them with the building unless some one takes the bolts lose and takes them away in pieces."

"Well I 'm coming back to your office, I'll be there within the hour maybe we can look up that Earl guy and see if we get any vibes".

"Okay said Ben I'll see you there." Jason got into his car and sat a moment trying to imagine the two little girls playing on this street and missing and never found. He counted years between the missing date of Anita and Christie, 1980 to 1986, six years apart and yet according to Jason's dreams they were still together. There were no storage tanks that he could see anywhere in the area. If they were in the ground no one would ever find them. But he remembered that one of the children said that they could hear people talking outside the can. He checked every room there was nothing big enough for two children with water in it except the boilers and they would have been sealed and filled with hot water. Jason began to visualize all of the bolts on the boiler units. The inside of the tanks would be loaded with the screws end of the bolts. He wondered if there might be a section of the boiler that could be removed but discounted the thought. The bolt heads were about one inch wide not a common wrench size or they would already be gone for scrap just as Ben had said.

He paused for another few seconds and reopened the folder to see if there was any other information about Mr. Norton.

"I'll be damned", he said out loud, it says here that Norton worked as a boiler maker for US Steel in the early eighties and had been laid off when the mills closed. "A boiler maker he repeated to himself while getting out of the car and nearly running back to the boiler room in building 210.

There it sat; a huge boiler with the reachable belly of it covered with asbestos. Jason knew without a doubt that the girls were inside. The rear side of the tank had ladder rings up to the top. Jason climbed up. On top of the round boiler there was a square plate about three feet by two feet. It had bolts about every two inches around the perimeter. Jason immediately got on the phone with Ben.

"Ben, it's me, I believe I've found the body's of the missing 5-year-olds. I'm going over to an auto supply place and get a set of wrenches to get into the boiler tank. Its sealed and I believe that after all these years it's still filled with water. With the valves rusted closed there's no way for it to drain. I'm going to take a look and see. If there are bodies inside you can get a warrant for that Norton guy.

He was a laid off boilermaker and he lived in this building during the time of the first missing child and two building's down from the second child's home and I wouldn't be surprised if his arrest wouldn't reveal more cases".

"Hey, good job. I'll be there by the time you're back."

"Ben … come alone for now, okay?"

"You know it."

By the time Ben arrived Jason was there and had removed all but two bolts. He was sweating from every pore and had discovered how to get them lose by pounding the wrench head with a hammer and turning counter clockwise at the same time. "Look out below "Jason said as he dropped the fifty pound plate to the concrete floor. The lid was off; the sealed tank was still nearly filled with black water.

"Get me your flashlight and a stick or a pole of some sort." The smell was horrifying and quickly filled the whole boiler room.

"You don't have to look any further Jason. I'd know that smell anywhere. You've found your children. Come down out of there and let me call it in for those that are trained to handle it from here. There's no need to witness what you may see, just come on down." Jason knew he was right. As he backed down the ladder, the realization of what he had just discovered struck in his heart.

"Oh my God Ben, he threw them in this hell hole to die and to never be found. What kind of man could this be?" Jason began to squeeze and shake the rusted metal ladder to the point that it started to bang loudly as if he were going to bring the whole boiler to the ground. He was furious and it showed in every muscle and expression that he could control. This case of missing or exploited children was solved. Once the bodies were identified the media would be on the case and report the names of the girls and the dates that they had become missing. Even though a mystery would be solved the public interest has been long gone. The memory of the two girls would be obscured by the many missing children that have been reported since the 1980's.

Before Ben could get onto his phone to call in the finding, Jason stopped him. "Ben, man, listen to me for a moment. You know how angry we can both get about what has occurred to these two young children?"

"Yeah" Ben responded. "There is no doubt about what I'd like to do to that creep, but remember we're not asleep. We are wide awake and in control enough to do the right thing".

"But something inside of me is telling me that I need to be standing right in front of that man when he is made to look down into that tank," he said while pointing up at what he had found.

"Those children are now spiritually free from being trapped in a tank filled with the water that drowned them more than 20 years ago. I don't think they came to us just to know that their killers have been arrested. I believe they want us to find satisfaction by giving us to opportunity to drag his ass into confession. I want to be a bigger part of the passing of judgment on behalf of these children. I'm asking you to not report the finding yet. I'm asking you to take me with you to pick him up. I'm asking you to let me help bring him back here where he can appreciate the sadness that he alone has caused."

"I'll tell you what," Ben said "I'll wait until tomorrow. We already have his address and from what I understand he owns a candy store and is now wheel chair bound due to diabetes. He won't be going anywhere of course, because he doesn't know the bodies have been found. After saying all of that, this is what we can do. I'll pick you up in the morning and we'll go to the man's home, pick him up and take him for a ride and see if we can get him to tell his side of the story. After that we've got to get the coroners office involved, how's that?" Ben asked.

"That's cool man. I'm going to put this lid back on for now. Thanks man. This means a lot to me since it was my dream that may bring this to a close. It's early yet, I'm going to go home and get some rest and await tomorrow. What time will you pick me up?"

"Let's make it about 10:30."

"Sounds good to me," Jason said. "Right now I feel sick at the stomach. I'm going home, take a shower and go to bed."

"I'm going back to the station to check a few things, and then I'm going to do the same," Ben said.

When Jason got home; at about 3:00 p.m., he found a note from Helen saying that she had called him several times and failed to get him to answer and that she and Sissy was going to a baby shower at a friends home in Wheeling West Virginia and would return tomorrow evening. Jason had experienced a day of a life time and had a story but no one to tell it to. So … just like he had told Ben he got his shower and found himself in bed before 3:30 p.m. His sleep came quickly and deep. So deep that there were no dreams, so deep that he did not toss or turn, so deep that he instantly gave up his body … to Oz. He slept but Oz had awakened. Oz slowly sat up on the side of the bed and took a very deep breath. Everything that Jason had experienced Oz was well aware of. He knew for example that the murderer of the 5-year-old that had been placed in a septic tank over in Youngstown, Ohio. Youngstown was less than a 90 minute drive. He knew that the murder of the two five-year-olds up is St. Clair Village now lived about twenty minutes away over in Arlington Heights. Oz got dressed and headed out to Youngstown. Oz had a plan. He craved revenge on behalf of the children that had visited Jason in his sleep. Oz had also listened to the children. And … he was more than angry. He was angrier than Jason could ever be capable of. He had viewed the computer where the sleeping screen still held information about the children and the names and addresses that had been provided by Ben. Even further he knew all that Jason knew. Like Jason he too wanted to react. Only Jason wanted to react and Oz was reacting. Oz arrived in Youngstown at approximately 5:15 p.m. The map finder on Jason's dashboard led him right to the door to be answered. When the door finally swung open Oz was pleased to be greeted by Dave himself.

"Hello David my name is Oz, we have a mutual friend that asked me to come by and visit you on my way back to Pittsburgh."

"Hello, how do you do?" Dave returned the greeting. "I'm pleased to meet you Mr. Oz"

"The reason that I stopped by is because our mutual friend mentioned that you were a modeling agent and I'm in the process of organizing talent shows for a local teenage modeling agency here in Youngstown and I was curious as to whether you maybe interested in structuring and directing the events. Of course it's a paid position. Or, I should say, very well paid position," Oz said

"I might. What does it pay?"

"Well it will be contingent upon the number of participants but somewhere between fifteen and twenty thousand plus other incentive," Oz answered with a smile. "I seen a Star Bucks Coffee House a couple of blocks down the street. Why don't we talk about it over a cup of brew?" Oz went on to say.

"Okay, that will be fine. I've got a couple of hours to kill before I'm due on a date. Give me a minute and I'll meet you there."

"All right good, I'll be waiting," Oz said while thinking this will be the last day that he will kill anything.

At Star Bucks David was more interested in how young the models will be than how much money he would make. Oz found himself doing more listening than explaining. The meeting wore Dave down. Oz offered to get Dave a refill before getting back onto the road to Pittsburgh. Dave accepted and the game began.

"I parked in the rear parking lot where I have a sample brochure of what we'd like to see happen. If you'd like to accompany me I can give it to you and we can get it all started."

"Okay, let's do that."

As they walked out the rear door to the parking lot Dave stumble a little and remarked.

"Wow. I thought caffeine was supposed to lift you up. I seem to be getting a little incoherent."

"Here let me help you a little. We're almost at my car," Oz said.

When they did reach Oz's car Oz let go of his arm as he fell onto the hood for support. Just then a man walked up from behind Oz and asked him what he was doing with Dave. Oz quickly looked at the man who also had reddish eyes and was wearing a name tag on his pocket which read 'Jordan Mitchell.'

"Hello Jordan" I'm about to help Dave to my car he seems to be drunk"

"What are you doing up in these parts Oz?" Jordan asked.

"Excuse me, you look vaguely familiar but more importantly I'd like to know how you know my name?" ask Oz.

My name in my current state of mind is Xe. I know you because I to live as a tool of God and I to have come to take Mr. David to find his resting place."

I'm sorry but Mr. Dave already has a date with me."

"It's okay, I know that when he is with you there is no doubt that he is in good hands. So, I will step aside and let the master do his work. Here is my better half's business card. Call me for breakfast next time your in these parts. Just ask for Jordan and I'll get the message," said Xe as he saluted Oz and walked away.

Dave was very woozy but still semi conscious and began to talk.

"Wow," he said, "I feel like a drunk. I must be getting sick." His voice began to slur. "I think I'm about to pass out."

"No you're not sick. I helped you out a little by putting ecstasy into your last cup of coffee. I'm sure you've heard of that. It's what rapist use to drug their potential victim. I manage to put an extra dose in your cup because I want you to take a ride back to Pittsburgh with me," Oz said while helping Dave onto the back seat of the car. He paused and turned his attention to Xe as he was walking away. "Hey," he said, "Call me some time at 412-853-0078 ask for Jason I to will get the message. You'll be hearing from me soon, in the mean time be safe."

"You got it." Oz turned back to Mr. David and said, "Just lye down and rest for a while. In a couple of hours it will have worn off and then we'll be able to talk about the most prideful model of your past. Susan Reed you remember Susan Reed don't you?"

Dave was now likened to a wet rag. The drug was in full affect. He was totally incoherent just as Oz had planned. On the way to Pittsburgh on a secluded road side parking area on route 79 south Oz pulled over and strapped Dave's wrist and ankles and placed him into the trunk of the car. The first part of his plan was complete, now he headed for Arlington Heights where Earl Norton of plan B was unknowingly enjoying his last day on earth.

It wasn't long before Oz pulled up in is Norton's drive way. He tapped his horn to get Earl's attention and he got out of the car and headed up the front steps. Day light was about to come to an end and Oz knew he had to step it up a little in order to get home before he would be missed.

Earl was sitting on the front stoop of his home used as a candy store. He seemed to be wheelchair bound due to a bout with diabetes or some other illness. What ever the illness it hadn't stopped his desire for children.

"Hey Earl, how are you doing? They told me you lived here. This is the first chance that I've had to stop by and say hello." Oz acted as if he'd known Earl all of his life.

"Hi, I'm sorry I don't remember your face."

"That's because we're getting older or I'm just not that memorable. Of course hanging at the Bell Lounge you never get a chance to see anybody's face that clearly. It was always dark in there."

"Ain't that the truth? I've spent a many a dollars in there picking up hussies for a shot and a beer."

"Yeah those were the days."

"I think the Bell has been closed for more than thirty years now hasn't it?"

"Yeah, I think so, "answered Oz who had never stepped foot in the place.

"Where did you say you were from?"

"I'm from the Southside but you would know me from hanging with the Saint Clair Village clan," answered Oz. "I just wanted to stop and say hello," Oz said as he turned away and started back to the car. He paused and looked back at Earl.

"Hey I've got a fifth of brandy in the car if you want a hit for old time's sakes your welcome to it."

"Hey you got the booze I got the glass. Bring it on in; I can have a couple of drinks with you, no doubt about it. I'm just waiting for the game to come on T.V. There's nobody here but me." That was music to Oz's ears. Plan B was in motion with plan A still bound and asleep in the trunk of his car.

The man's place was a pig sty but bad housekeeping was the least of his bad habits. Oz sat down and waited for a glass.

"Here's to the good old days even though I'm only fifty I've made a dent in the good life, how about you?"

"Yeah me to," answered Oz. "Do you still rape little girls?" Oz asked. The question totally threw Earl from one mode to another.

At first he responded with, "Yeah, when I can, blind, cripple or crazy, white or black from eight to eighty. You know the old saying," Earl remarked.

After saying what he said and holding up his glass of liquor for a tap, he realized that Oz's expression was no longer showing that of an old friend. "I've had my share of females," he said with a much less bragging tone of voice.

"I asked you if you are still raping babies and stuffing the bodies in a boiler tank." The man's face dropped to an expression of panic.

"Don't just sit there, answer my question stupid. Are … you … still … killing babies?" Oz was panting with anger. "Well, answer me!"

"I don't know what you're talking about."

"Sure you do. You know what I'm talking about. You know exactly what I'm talking about. I'm talking about Anita and Chrisie.

"I'm about to call the police. You had better get out of here right now."

"Here we go again. Do you know how many times I've been threatened by cowards in an attempt to weasel out of a chance to satisfy your debt?"

Oz quickly stood up and grabbed the rear handles of his wheel chair and dumped him onto the floor.

"What's wrong with you, can't you see I'm a cripple?"

"Bull shit, get up off the floor and walk with me to your death!" Oz said. "Get up now!"

"I can't. I can't get up I'm cripple."

Oz grabbed a nearby phone cord and wrapped it around his neck and began to drag him towards the door.

'Okay, Okay I'll get up."

Earl slowly got up to his knees and then without warning jump up onto his feet and charged at Oz like a bear. He was growling and roaring in his own attempt to kill or be killed. After Oz was driven against the wall hard enough to take down the average man he pushed back and wrapped the cord around Earl and in one sweeping motion pulled him down onto the floor again. After laying him on his back he continued to bind him with the cord until he was unable to do anything but talk.

"Okay, what do you want? You've got me now what are you going to do with me?"

With Earl now helplessly bound Oz walked around him a couple of times looking at the man with despise.

Earl began to bravely talk to Oz.

"You can't hurt me now. Where were you when you could have prevented the deaths of those children? Huh? Where were you then Mr. Oz? Were you somewhere blessing a meal or preaching about salvation. I'm a weak man Oz, how about you? Are you strong enough to stop the lust? Huh, or are you just another pretender. Your kind is always a little too late. Can you bring them back from the dead like Jesus, or can you just tell us that it's an abomination of God and just walk away until judgment day?"

"No, I can't do much of anything. I'm not God, but I can guarantee that you will never kill again."

"Yeah, well I wasn't going to kill again anyway. So you are still too late. Let me tell you how many kids I've molested. Do you want to know? Huh, do you? Ten or fifteen that's how many; maybe more. Do you know how many kids I've stuffed in that boiler? Huh, do you? Six; Oz there is six luscious little darlings all of them were mine. Would you like to know how I started, why I started, when I started? How old I was the first time I did it? Who might have done it with or to me? Would you like to know these things or do you want to just kill me and never know the mentor. Did you know I was catholic Oz? Did you know that? Did you know that when I was very young I learned to play with the dick of my trusted priest? Did you know that? It's about lust Oz. It's about the grooming and setting of a mind. How would peon angelic guardians like you and your hand full of fools stop the acts of selfishness and the conquest of the innocent? Acts that give us the ultimate pleasure of being like a god. We have the power of turning down the plea of a child that's begging to live or a mother or a father begging to get their child back. We have the power to steal the virginity of a baby while God watches and fools like you pursue and save sinners with chance after chance to sin again. Do you know what it's like to crave the act, to achieve the act or the sorrow that we feel after the act is over? Have you ever felt the fear of being exposed? Or what it feels like to put yourself into the hands of Jesus, just to start it all over again when the opportunity arrives. No, you can't hurt me. You can take my life, in fact, most of the time during my cycle of pleasure and pain I wish I were dead or better yet, never born. So hurry it up Oz, take this one life and look for another and another until you find the cause. I hate what ever caused my filthy life. Kill it for me. I don't know from whence it came. I just know that it comes and goes. And just as God enjoys when good things happen, the mentor of pedophilia finds satisfaction when the lust becomes overwhelming uncontrollable to the point of yielding to his temptation."

"More bullshit Earl, you have had plenty of time to pacify your own selfish lust with stories and justifiable reasons of why you can't stop. There is no mentor, if there were, where is he now? Why can't he rescue you? How does he speak to you? How has he shown you the way? What is his reward? On second thought, no, don't answer me; just tell him that you are on your way to hell. We have no intentions of letting the disease of pedophilia and murder run ramped while baby killers like you enjoy life for whatever it has to offer. If there is such a thing as a mentor for pedophiles and he is human let him know that the children are accusing, judging and sentencing them to the penalty of a horrid death. With the on slot of darkness, Oz carried the bound and gagged predator to his car and threw him into the back seat. After a fifteen minute drive he arrived at 210 Bonifay Street.

During the time that it took Oz to capture both men Helen had become concerned that Jason hadn't returned her calls and contacted Ben asking him to check on Jason and to make sure that he was all right. After the pleasantry of greetings, Ben informed Helen that the two of them had met earlier in the day and was suppose to meet again in the morning. From what you're saying I think I might know where he is. I'm going to go check and I'll call you back as soon as I know something. Ben hung up the phone and headed for Bonifay Street.

In the mean time oz had taken Mr. Earl into the boiler room that he had known so well more than twenty years ago. Still well bound and gagged Earl could give no resistance. Even so, he still seemed to be tormenting Oz with his eyes and what appeared to be a grin upon his face. Oz climbed the metal ladder and set the lid of the boiler storage tank aside. He descended and with Earl over his shoulder made his way back to the top. The tank was about six foot tall at the bottom center with the water level down about a foot from the top. As Earl finally realized what Oz was about to do he began to wiggle and move in everyway that he could. He was no longer smiling, now he was frantic and trying to make as much noise as he could. Oz slid him into the tank feet first and made sure that he still remained out of the water from his shoulders and up. Oz then tide Earl in such away preventing him from sinking any further into the black liquid grave site. He paused for a moment while looking into Earl's eyes face-to-face and almost nose to nose.

"This will be good for you Mr. Earl. You get a chance to spend some time with the children that you so cold bloodedly murdered. And I'll get the satisfaction of knowing you won't be dead when I leave. But by the time I come back and close down the lid you will have given a lot of thought to those below you. On top of all of this I have a surprise for you. You're going to have a new friend standing right in front of you. You and he can share stories about how powerful you've both been among babies. While I go get him from the trunk of the car you can decide weather you want him facing you or behind you with an erection or should I say, I'm asking you, would you like to be behind him? The choice is yours. After all, this is your boiler tank," Oz said while descending again down the metal ladder. Before he reached the ground another light other than his own lit up the boiler room. It was Ben.

"What are you doing Jason? I thought we were going to do the right thing and pick him up tomorrow morning for an arrest. You know I can't let you do this."

"Do I know you sir? You look like Ehsa but you sound like a woman."

"Don't play with me Jason, this is no game," Ben said as he slowly walked a little closer to who he thought was Jason.

"You've been taken over haven't you Jason or should I call you Oz?"

"Call me what ever you like, but I'm saying to you, sure you can, you can let me do this. In fact there's no way you can stop me. So leave and let me get on with my task."

"Who do you have up there in the tank Jason?"

"It's Earl, and stop calling me Jason, he's at home and fast asleep. You know Earl, don't you Ehsa? He's a child killer. Earl has a debt to pay and by order of the children that he has murdered, he must pay now. So please, leave me to my task in peace."

Ben drew is weapon and loosely held it down against his right leg.

"Are you going to shoot me? Ehsa are you not a stronger being than this Ben."

Ben was puzzled and very much undecided on what to say or do.

Oz said, "I wasn't going to harm him. I was going to leave him here for a while to relish the pleasure of being with his victims. I haven't touched him other than a couple of telephone cords to keep him from hurting himself."

"Wait; stay right where you are!" Ben demanded as Oz or Jason walked away from him toward the exit door of the boiler room. "Where do you think you're going?"

"Earl has a new friend that wants to join him."

"Wait, don't tell me … Mr. Reed, right?" Ben asked.

"Yes, how did you know?" responded Oz.

"Oh man Jason you've really put me on the spot. I know we've talked about coming to the aid of children. But these two children have been dead for more than twenty years."

"Oh yeah, how many children do you think are in that tank?" Oz asked.

"I assumed there are two."

"Well there are at least six, with the most recent being just eight months ago."

Ben was silent as he put his gun back into its holster. After a log pause he said,

"Okay, I'm walking away Jason or better yet, Oz. I haven't even seen Jason since this morning. This one is yours."

Oz watched as Ben left the building and drove away.

"Well Mr. Dave should be awake by now," he said to himself. "I'll introduce him to his new friend in the tank and get back home to get me and Jason some rest." When Oz opened the trunk of the car, David was awakening but still incoherent. Oz lifted him out of the trunk and onto his shoulder.

"Well Mr. Dave welcome back to the world. You've finally got a chance to see how it feels under the influence of your own medicine."

David's mouth remained taped shut but his eyes danced around in fear as he moaned and mumbled with his face towards Oz's lower back. Up the metal ladder for what Oz hoped would be the last time. Earl was, of course, patiently waiting without a choice.

"Look what I've brought you. It's a bird of the feather."

Once he lowered David into the tank facing Earl he removed the duck tape from their mouths. They both immediate began to express rage with profanity and the same questions. Oz formally introduced them.

"Dave; child rapist and murderer, I want you to meet Earl; child rapist and murderer. And of course along with each other you have the corpse of six small murdered children. I don't guess you need to know their names. They are free now but will entertain both of your minds for a few hours or days. And then do you know what I'm going to do? I'm going to come back and; if you are still alive I will take you both down to the Monongahela River for a nice swim. I'm hoping that you both will have met your maker by then."

Both men continued to deny, complain and plea for their lives.

Oz sat on the far end of the tank facing them in silence.

"I'm sorry," he said, speaking to the children in the tank in a solemn voice with his head held low to his chest. "I have no way to bring any of you back to this life. I know the pain and loneliness that you've endured and the pain of missing you that your memories have caused to many of the living. If I had my way there would have been no threat from the likes of these two predatory beasts. I'm sorry that I did not hear your cries or your prayers. I'm sorry that I didn't come to your rescue when the pain and confusion was still inside of your bodies, while you were alive and on your way to gloom. I did not hear your voices," Oz said as tears ran down his face. "I don't know why the thousand of you that have been allowed to be deceived by false and selfish men and sons of men. But your revenge has become the passion of my existence. I won't stop pursuing those that have violated you until the cure is found or I have the pleasure of hearing each and every evil heart come to a stand still. Prayer has obviously let you down. As their prayers have led you into their dens of selfish pleasure; your own prayers have fallen short. Again, I must say, I don't know why."

With hate overwhelming Oz at every level he slowly raised his head and looked through his tears at both men that were standing in the fluids of what was left of their victims. They had silenced themselves to hear what Oz had to say. Cowardly fear for their own lives had caused evil to vacate them and their bodies. Now they were just ordinary men of no spiritual substance or hope of life. They were both still standing and breathing but dead in every other way. Again the thrill of revenge had escaped Oz just as it had for others like him when the time of reckoning was about to inflict its final blow. Oz wiped away his tears and descended to the floor below leaving his two predators to relish what ever the sting that death has to offer. The tank was alive below them with an unknown energy, unknown to even Oz. It absorbed the flesh like an acid. It may be all in the mind of Oz, but as he walked out of the building strange sounds filled the air. Not the sound of men screaming or begging for life; instead the sounds were like none he had heard in heaven or earth. The sound was an expression of redemption even though words like redemption have no sound. There was a frightening rumble followed by a loud sign of relief. Vengeance did belong to God. Oz got into his car and glanced over at the boiler room door from which he had just come. In the darkness everything went completely silent and motionless. The sight represented a perfect view of what should be titled the end. Oz started the car and headed back to Jason. He knew that when the spirits of children suffer so does God. He reasoned that God feels better now. He thought heavily of what had happened and began to allow the spirit of Jason to seep into his mind.

* * * * *

Author's insert about the coming chapter and its ramifications:

Let's pause for a moment and think about the huge number of violent pedophiles that are nested inside of households all across America. Is there a profile that fits in a way that we can be forewarned of the pending actions whenever their opportunity arrives? Remember opportunity is a very key word when it comes to the safety of your child. To put a child age zero to ten alone and with enough time in the company of a child molester is equal to allowing him to run across the freeway until he or she is struck by a car. It's just a matter of time. Child molesters are opportunist. They are aware that the consequences of their acts can be devastating to their own well-being. They often manage to resist their urge of satisfying their sexual appetite until they think that they can get away with the crime. Some may never enact their sexual craving because the risk of getting caught out weighs their lust. Let's call them 'Potential'.

These men and women are probably the least harmful to children until opportunity allows them to strike. Of course, the biggest threats to all children are the outright rapist. They have no intentions of sacrificing their desire to sexually violate, molest and even murder their victims. Often with this group of rapists, time is not of the essence, and at other times they are so overwhelmed with lust for children that they are willing to risk their lives for the relief that success brings. These are the predators that instill fear in men, women and children.

Again, what determines their success is "opportunity." They are known to have stalked children for weeks and some have even snatched babies from the arms of their mothers. They've also been known to waste no time raping a child that's been left alone in a restroom or on a playground; even during social events when the parents aren't vigilant. They have been commonly known to physically harm the child even after they've completed their orgasm.

Somewhere in between these two predators lies what can be called the in-house pedophile. These are the most common and by far the most damaging in the sense of spreading the disease. These are usually family members or trusted friends. Their victims have been known to number very high in their sexually active lifetime. That number can actually equate to millions of children in any given generation. And... they tend to create a cycle of reoccurring molestations due to the fact that they are often loved by the victim and their victim's clueless family members. They are generally quickly forgiven to avoid embarrassment to the family if they promise and swear that they will never do it again. Ironically every time they do it they have no intentions of doing it again; at least until they get another opportunity.

This is a description or profile of a child molester/pedophile:

- *They are often tall, short and in between.*
- *They have been known to be thin, overweight and obese.*
- *They are sometimes well educated scholars and third grade drop outs.*
- *They are white, black, Hispanic, Native American, Asians, Oriental and, as far as we know, mostly humans.*
- *They live in rich housing communities, public housing and the average neighborhood.*
- *They are lesbian, gays and straight.*
- *They are alcoholics, drug users and clean upstanding citizens; both male and female.*
- *Some are employed but they are often unemployed.*
- *Some have an arrest record; while others have never been arrested. Sadly some will never be arrested.*

The description can go on and on. Again, opportunity seems to be their commonality. However, after saying all of the above, there are a few characteristics that may stand out.

We know for example that they all seem to be self-oriented to the point that the only life they can relate to is their own. I guess you could say that they are the center of their own attraction. They rehearse until an opportunity allows them to perform. Pedophiles seem to never participate in open conversation concerning child abuse; it's as if they fear being recognized. Many previously sexually abused women claim that they can recognize a pedophile when they see one; that there are things that only they exhibit, yet this is inconclusive statistically.

†

75% of sexual predators are younger than 35. About 80% are of normal intelligence or above.

— Profiles from the FBI Academy and the National Center for Missing and exploited children

†

For the vast majority of children victimizers in the State prisons, the victim was someone they knew before the crime. 1/3 had committed their crime against their own child, about 50% had a relationship with the victim as a friend, acquaintance, or relative other than an offspring, about 1 in 7 reported the victim to have been a stranger to them.

— BJS Survey of State Prison Inmates, 1991

†

"God's greatest gift to man is our children. Sigmund Freud once stated: "I cannot think of any need in childhood as strong as the need of a father's protection." It is the obligation of every man, because we are all fathers, to protect our children from anyone that would rob them of their innocence."

— Douglas Huggins,
Businessman, retired transit worker

CHAPTER FIVE

The Groomer:

Oz had one of the most emotionally disturbing confrontations of his life. Victoria moved herself into his sleeping mind with cunningness and control. Her mood as an informant had changed into a mode of reliving a distorted story of romance between her as a child and an adult named Gene. She used her power of persuasion to maneuver Oz into a confused state of mind by telling her story of a romance that she defends as not only acceptable but as one that every child should have. Ultimately she convinced Oz to rethink his feelings about his approach to pedophilia. Her story started with a man named Gene that lived within her household. Each day he came home at 5:30 p.m. from work.

"That was five hours before my mother returned from her work day at the hospital. Early in our relationship he made me feel much more special than my younger sister or brother. He brought me packs of gum and candy nearly everyday. On my seventh birthday he brought me a birthday cake and a wrapped gift that he said I couldn't open until my sister Regina and my brother Randy were in bed. It was a winter night and it got totally dark at 6:30 p.m. We ate and Regina and Randy were put to bed by 7 p.m.

Mister Gene invited me into my mommy's room to open my present. It was a child's makeup kit with lipstick and eye shadow. He told me that I could play with the makeup but that I needed to put it away and go to my own bed before mommy got home at 10:30 p.m. On the days that followed he brought me other things like nylon stockings and a small bra so that I could pretend to be an adult. I was very special and he treated me better than the others. Eventually I was allowed to wear my makeup and watch T.V. with Mr. Gene for a couple of hours each night. One night while I was taking a bath Mr. Gene came into the bathroom and began took out his wiener and turned towards me with his robe open. A few days later he did it again, this time he shook himself and rubbed it and played with his pubic hair while peeing into the toilet and talking to me. I remember looking at him as he shook it. I watched while I sat in the tub naked. After a few more occasions he kind of caught me looking at it and said something like, you better stop looking at this as he shook it and done his ritual of playing with the hair above it. I began to await his entry and position myself so that I could see it better when he came into the bathroom.

One night he peed and stood there pulling on it until it began to grow and stick straight out. I was amazed at the way it looked and changed size. He stood in front of me for what seem like a long time just rubbing him self. I felt very strange inside. I couldn't take my eyes off of it. He asked me if I wanted to touch it and I shook my head yes. He just stood there smiling telling me I could feel it as long as I wanted to and at any time. After a few minutes he pulled it away and called me a bad little girl. For a couple of days he didn't come into the bathroom. I thought I had done something wrong and I wouldn't get to see it again. The next day I got out of the tub and dried off and was walking from the bathroom to my bedroom when he called out my name and told me to; 'Come here. Close the door,' and I did. 'You've been a really good girl,' he said. And then he told me, 'Tomorrow I'll bring you home anything you want. Just tell me what it is. Okay?"

"Okay," I answered. He was lying under the sheet. He patted the bed and told me to come and sit on the bed and think about what I may want. He lay back down on his back with his head propped up on the pillow. While talking he was rubbing his wiener and it was sticking straight up making the sheet appear like a white tent. I tried not to look because I thought he didn't want me to. And then he told me to look at it. He said it hadn't seen me in a while and it needed a hug.

"Hug it," he said. "Give it a big hug for Gene." Then he pushed the sheet off of it and exposed it. It seemed much bigger than before. It was making me feel even stranger than before and when I touched it I got a little dizzy.

"Go head hug it. It won't hurt you I promise." I laid the side of my face against it and felt it all over. It seemed to have magical powers. Touching it made me feel so good. While I was touching it he was touching it to. I remember resting my head just above his knee where I fell off to sleep. I awoke for a moment when he was carrying me to my room. When I woke up the next morning I wanted to see it again and touch it. I think it had become my new favorite plaything. I couldn't wait to see it again. Days went by without him coming into the bathroom. I finally got out of the tub one night and peeked into his room, through a crack in the door. He was lying there naked watching TV.

"Who is that?" he asked.

"It's me," I answered.

"What do you want sugar?"

"Nothing," I answered. I stood there a while until I asked if I could come in. He said yes and covered himself up from the waist down.

"What's up sugar pie? I don't have any candy for you. Your little brother and sister ate it all up."

"That's okay," I said.

"Come up here on the bed," he said and continued to look at the book he had in his hand.

"What's that?" I asked him while pointing at his wiener.

"You know him. That's your friend, Wicky," he said without looking up from his book.

"I touch him?" I asked.

"I'm going to read my book you guys can do whatever you want, just don't disturb me," he said. I cuddled up with Wicky, as he called him. He had put down his book and I think he went to sleep. I went to sleep, too.

Later when he was carrying me to my room he whispered that he wasn't going to ever tell anybody about me and my new friend.

It will be a secret for you and Wicky and nobody else. Sometimes I asked to play with him and Mr. Eugene would say no not tonight. Other times he would say that Wicky needs a kiss first."

Oz listened to Victoria's story and heard it in his mind ten times over. This pedophile was different from the rest. He molded his victim into thinking that he was servicing her at her request. This one was not about violent rape and murder. This type of child molester was shrewd and cunning and able to outwit the seven to eleven year age group. He kept himself out of the danger of being exposed by the child, especially young boys.

This tactic was as safe as molestation could get. They became secure after convincing the child that he wouldn't tell on them no matter what. And no matter what the child would maintain his or her appreciation by protecting what they believe to be a love affair filled with a storybook romance.

Oz was disturbed and very confused about the resolve of this infraction. An eye for an eye has been his way to repay for the taking of a child's spirit through the forceful pain on rape and murder. How could he intervene and what would he choose as a consequence.

Could it be possible that a good man may be rejected and asked not to interfere? Oz decided to place the complicated matter into the mind of Jason. Oz had learned that there was a threshold between the end of his dreams and the beginning of Jason's.

When it was nearly time for Jason to repossess his physical body and mind Oz concentrated on Victoria; causing it to be a story that Jason carried into his sub-conscience before waking up the next morning. Jason woke up to a troubled heart just as Oz had anticipated. He clearly remembered every part of his dream and the entire story of Victoria's love affair with Eugene. Jason had the burden of having more details than Oz. For example, Jason was aware that she was still very much in love with and still sexually involved with her mother's husband and obviously has been for nearly eight years. She has had no other lover nor has she pursued the thought.

Jason reasoned that to intervene in anyway would be offensive to Victoria; yet he felt a certain amount of responsibility in bringing this blatant act of child abuse to the authorities. His first thought was to approach the mother but he had no way to confirm his accusation without the input of Victoria. For him to say he dreamed it all would simply appear to be ludicrous. He called Ben and informed him of this newly exposed situation that has leaded him into an unsolvable crisis. After listening to Jason about Victoria's story he responded with several possibilities but none that fit as a solution. After a very lengthy discussion Ben suggested that he should call Mack down in Washington and that he may be able to access the right approach to this kind of abuse. Jason did just that. After speaking with Mack about his most recent dreams/nightmares he brought up the subject of Victoria. The minute Jason brought up the name of Victoria Mack interrupted.

"Don't tell me you dreamed about her too. I dreamed of her three nights in a row and no, I'm sorry for interrupting you tell me about your dream first and I'll tell you mine.

Jason told Mack the details of his Victoria dream and expressed his concern that these types of pedophiles do just as much damage to children as a violent rapist. "They certainly disrupt the foundation of family trust and stability."

"I agree, but I'd hate to have to be the one that goes into the home of a struggling family to tell them that the only bread winner they have is a well-loved or even hated pedophile. My dream was a little different than yours," Mack continued to say. "Victoria told me that she wants to marry her father when she grows up. She's convinced that her dad loves her and wants to take her away to a place of make believe. She even said she wants to have his baby. Jason, she's only twelve years old."

"The Victoria in your dream is twelve?" Jason asked.

"Yeah and she kind of boosted that she's almost thirteen. The problem with all this is that she truly thinks that she is her father's romantic mate. I asked her what has your mother said about this and she responded that my daddy hates my mommy. Her father is a fifty-eight-year-old man that works on city council."

"That's strange my Victoria mentioned that her dad was a fireman," Jason said. After further conversation and a few more comparisons they agreed that they have the same Victoria just two different stories. The same type of sexual relationship and two totally different fathers; in fact, after recollecting the details of their dreams this relationship occurred in two different cities. Mack's dream, though he lives near Washington D.C. took place in Pittsburgh. Jason's dream had taken place in Tacoma Park, Maryland.

"Did your Victoria mention her father's name?" Jason asked.

"Yes, as a matter of fact she did. She kept calling him Eugene but she said her real father's name was Elbert Winston. Has Ben had a Victoria dream?"

"No, he said that he hadn't. I'm going to call Charles down in Florida to see if he has as soon as I get off of the phone with you. You said she mentioned that she was twelve, did she happen to say how long this Eugene or Elbert guy has been her lover?"

"No, but it's all so confusing and tangled up that we may never dream of her again. And another thing, I'm not absolutely sure which was her father, at the end of this dream she said she was pregnant by her true love, her father."

After Jason finished talking to Mack he called Ben back and brought him up to date about Mack's Victoria dream and asked him out of his own curiosity for information about any recently missing eleven or twelve-year-old that has ties in Pittsburgh. Her father's name is Eugene or Elbert Winston mothers name Marjorie …

After a few hours of on-line investigation Ben got right back to Jason and informed him that he discovered that there was such a child. She was missing and she had been get pregnant according to the family doctor that had given her a physical just a few days before she came up missing. The mother reportedly remarked that the child was very excited about the aspect of having the baby. Though this real life mother was quoted as saying that the daughter refused to reveal who the father was, she and her husband, Elbert, had decided not to question her about who the father might be but instead help her decide whether she should immediately get an abortion.

According to her parents she wanted her baby and decided to run away and supposedly kept the father of the baby a secret.

Now, as crazy as all this seems there are additional twists. Number one, the mother says that her child has had no obvious access to a boyfriend or any male other than Catholic Church activities on Sundays. Other than that she is at school or home. So, go ahead. What else happened with Victoria's secret?" Jason asked Ben to keep him informed if anything else came up …

In the mean time he told Ben that he was about to talk to Charles and inquire if he had a Victoria dream. We've learned that our Victoria is letting us know that she has been a willing participant without regrets, and that she has been groomed and petted until she was molded into believing she's in love and initiates the sexual contact. Charles and I believe that this type of loving pedophile will be nearly impossible to expose."

* * * * *

Jason and Ben had missed each others calls most of the day. When they did finally catch up wit each other by phone they each had a story that couldn't wait. "I need to give you an update on Victoria and the similar dream that Charles has been having down D.C."

"No wait; this is more than a dream. I have a case that turned on the hate of even the gentlest man at the precinct."

"Okay you go first, I'm all ears," said Jason, "That sounds good, let me tell you this; every since I've started questioning my fellow officers about child molestation and murders in the Pittsburgh area; everyone has made me aware of every case that's on the books, both past and present.

"Listen to this, a couple of days ago a four-month-old infant that had been brought into children's hospital and it puzzled everybody. The baby was very sick and was non-responsive to everything they attempted in the emergency room. After a few days the baby died.

The autopsy revealed that the baby died from complications from what appeared to be stemming from a venereal disease.

"We were called in to try and determine who the child contracted this from. We questioned both parents and discovered that the man was just a boyfriend that had just been released from prison after serving five years on a child molestation rap. The mother had dated him before he went to jail; she broke up with the abusive father of her children and brought home the ex-con Ed Robinson aka, Blue. She said she felt safe with him, and he was big enough to keep the kids' father out of her life!

"Well we determined that Blue had been asked to watch the baby for a few hours while she went to the hairdresser. There were no signs of sexual abuse. Not even a scratch anywhere and yet this baby is dead. We examined every possibility, but it just didn't make sense. We drilled the father beyond imagination. He had taken a lie detector test and passed it twice!

"The doctors suggested that maybe the mother passed something down to the baby. They gave the mother every test possible all with negative results. The doctors were stuck on the fact of the unknown cause of death.

"I watched as the couple walked away needing each other more then ever. I felt so bad for her I even thought to myself that it's a good thing she has someone to lean on in a time like this. Just before exiting the building she turned and waved with a couple of fingers. Blue turned also and sadly waved, saying thank you for doing a thorough job for my girl. With that last word, they were out of my sight.

"I finally got the message in my heart that everyone who has a record and appears very suspect can't be tried and convicted, and that there will be times that an innocent man is pre-judged and found clean of responsibility. I actually felt bad, because we all thought of him to be the killer of the baby. You know how we roll; I wanted that sucker bad.

That night I went home thankful for our justice system." Ben paused for a moment as if not knowing how to complete the story. "Now listen to me, I fell off to sleep after at least an hour of soul searching and regretful thoughts that I may have pre-judged not only this guy Blue but a number of men and maybe even took the law into my own hands in cases in the past. I drifted off to sleep and immediately heard the crying of a child. The child was lying at the foot of my bed. I tried to shake it off and I slightly awakened; only to doze off again with the baby now screaming at the top of its lungs. I sat up and gave in to the urge to pick up the baby or something; I didn't know just what. I don't know how but I recognized that the baby was the child that had died. I didn't know what to do. I held the baby close to my chest and rocked her gently back and forth. She screamed louder, I pushed back the baby's tears and wiped her cheeks with my finger. She arched her back and turned her head from side to side trying to feed on my finger as it came close to her mouth. My God, I said, you're hungry. I took the knuckle of my first finger and started toward her chin, immediately she tried to pacify her hunger and feed on my knuckle. The infant sucked a few times and seemed to die in my arms. I can't begin to explain my fear that I may have let a baby die in my arms. The dream repeated itself three times, each time the infant died after a few sucks on my knuckle. Thank God a baby can't die from sucking. I couldn't figure out why she kept dying and then it hit me, she must have ingested something from my hand. Jason, then the whole message became clear to me that the baby had ingested whatever it was that killed her. There wouldn't be any bruises or lesion, not even a scratch. My God, I thought, that bastard committed himself orally to the hungry infant.

I got up, dressed and headed to the parents residence.

On the way I remembered that we had not had the man tested for any venereal disease, only the mother. I was squeezing my steering wheel so tightly on the drive there that my knuckles had begun to turn pale and you know how unusual that is for black man. I was imploding inside with hatred. I knew this was exactly what happened there was no doubt in my mind. I pulled into her driveway and sat for a moment trying to decide whether I should call for back up or not. I calmed myself a little by realizing that I've got the creep and he'll be put away for life. Then I'm not sure what happened. I remember ringing the door bell and going in. She answered the door and let me in but she didn't recognize me.

"Is Blue here," I asked.

"Yes" she answered, "he's sleeping in the back room.

"He doesn't sleep with you?"

"What kind of question is that sir," she asked angrily."

"I'm sorry, I just was wondering how he has a venereal disease and you don't."

"Sir, I don't know what you're talking about but I'm telling you now; I'm reporting you to your superiors. Now please leave!"

"Miss I'm not here for a friendly visit, I need to talk to him right now. You can tell whoever you want later, but right now he's gonna answer my questions. So let's go back and talk to him," I said as I pushed past her. She followed me back pointing to the room where he was sleeping. I opened the door and something seemed to take over my soul. "I'm going to try and tell you exactly what I said and done. I grabbed him off of the bed with more strength than I thought I had. I said, 'you piece of shit why didn't you tell us you had a venereal disease, they could have saved the baby!' I didn't know I could hurt her he blurted out," he said. I had already lifted him off of his feet and I slammed him against the walls so hard that it shook the room. "I didn't mean to hurt her," he said.

"You let that baby suck you when she wanted to be fed; you dirty low life sack of shit." I threw him down on his back and cuffed him at his waste line.

"I'm sorry … I'm sorry," he kept saying. I glanced over at the mother; her face had dropped in disbelief. Her mouth and eyes were struck with shock. I worried that she was about to faint.

"This man sexually violated your baby by feeding her his penis in the place of her bottle." She just stood there in a trance. "Did you hear what I said? This man is responsible for your daughter's death."

"I didn't mean it, I was being stupid. I didn't know it would kill her, I swear to God I wouldn't have hurt a little baby." I took out my nine and held it to his head.

"I should blow your f—king head off and end your stinking life right now."

"No please, it was an accident" he said crying like a baby. Then without warning he rose up and crashed his head against my chest and up into my chin knocking my nine to the floor and me right behind it. I wrestled with him for a couple of minutes and gained position on top of him while holding his cuffed hands up around the back of his neck.

"Your going to jail for a long time Mr. Blue, I'm going to see to that" I said. Suddenly his eyes grew wide open as he was looking beyond me over my left shoulder. I briefly turned to see what he was looking at. She was standing with my nine pointing at Blue's face. She fired three times. I could feel the force of the bullets blowing past my head and making contact with Blue's face. Flesh and blood and pieces of bones exploded everywhere letting the cuffs that I had holding him behind his neck pull into my lap. His head was gone just like that. I quickly stood up as she walked closer and emptied my gun into his chest. It was over within a few second. Blue was blown to pieces beyond recognition. She turned and faced me while passing me my empty gun. I wanted to applaud her but instead I took the gun from her and hugged her at the same time. I understand I said. This all happened early this morning. Now ... tell me your story."

"No wait," Jason said. "What do you thinks gon'na happen to the mother?"

"I had to arrest her, but I'm sure she'll be fine. To me she saved my life; she is a hero. Now tell me about what you were going to say."

"I'll tell you about it at another time. After hearing your story it seems that all pedophiles will be difficult to expose. If the baby hadn't died we may have never known that he was performing or should I say acting out his evil thoughts. More importantly these dreams we are having have become a very important part of our lives. We all seem to have been chosen as some sort of medium to expose violent sexual abuse against children that have deceased. It's sort of after the fact. I believe that Victoria's stories may make us refocus a little on exposing the disease long before it becomes fatal for a child emotionally or physical. Right now there are ten of us that acknowledge that we have been chosen. It seems we will need thousands to put a dent in finding a cure of some sort. Let me tell you one more thing before I let you go and get some rest. I've kind of been made aware that we all have dual counterparts that not only exist during our dreams, but have actually taken over our bodies until they have fulfilled their own objectives of revenge. I know that my counterpart or split person is Oz and yours is Ehsa, Charles is Jax, Mack's is Clay and I know a few more but I'm not sure how I know. I am sure that each of them is ferocious and set on vengeance that may put each of us in jail. We've got to come together and determine how to protect ourselves against the possibilities of getting seriously injured or imprisoned."

Ben responded with a calm,

"Yeah man your right, we've got to get control. Bring us together Jason. Maybe we can make a difference somehow, even more importantly, maybe before the kids are harmed instead of after" Ben's voice had broken down to that of a man that understood the right of our children to be safe and sound and to be loved not used. "How do we get to them before they're corrupted by their own foolish lust? Where do we start? Or do you think we should just turn it over to Oz and Ehsa or Clay?"

"Probably both. Our message is weakened by human compassion. The likes of Oz deliver a clear and precise message, that being, 'touch the children and answer to God'. Let's try to educate the mothers to keep vigilance 24 hours a day. I guess it's the old 'ounce of prevention pound of the cure'. To pedophiles all we can offer is the cure of Oz," Jason said he hung up on Ben.

†

While nearly 70% of those serving time for violent crimes against children are white. Whites accounted for only 40% of those imprisoned for violent crimes against adults.

— BJS Survey of State Prison Inmates

†

50% of reported child molestation involved the use of physical force and child molesters produce as much visible physical injury as rapists.

— Dr. Gene Abel in a National Institute of Mental Health Study

†

"As responsible adults, we cannot continue to live with our morals intact if we do not properly address the issues of child pornography and child sexual abuse. We cannot afford to standby and let our in affective court system let convicted offenders of go free to strike again and again after a period of time behind bars. These words, Protection, Intervention, and Solution, need to take on a new meaning with regard to their usage in conjunction with those who violate the law and prey upon helpless children. The Protection has to be everlasting, the intervention has to be swift and consistent, and the solution has to be permanent."

— Rocco B. Reynolds,
Retired army ranger/current State employee

CHAPTER SIX

By November Jason's dreams had moved to another level, keeping Oz busy for 3-4 nights a week covering a much larger geographical area than any of his previous dreams. Oz/Jason traveled from Cleveland to New York in pursuit of positively identifying violent pedophiles. While Oz represented an end to their murdering predators, Jason began to spend more time volunteering to bring awareness to the threat of pedophilia. During the day Jason, Mack, Charles and Benn contemplated ways to bring potential pedophiles to the eye opening reality that their sickness should be dealt with and not tampered with. They constantly communicated the need to expose the sexual hunger for a child as a life and happiness ending violation that disrupts everyone concerned, simply put; it should not be accepted or tolerated by love ones or the conscience with-in themselves.

On December 12th the inevitable happened, all five men dreamed identical dreams. The dreams were finalized by each angel crying out in extreme pain in the outer limits of anger. In the city of Chicago three pedophiles set up a good man by the name of Jordan Mitchell whose angelic name is Xe. Jason had not met Jordan Mitchell or any of the five angels outside of his own circle of friends. Just like the others, his dream of that night was as clear as being there in reality. Jason's Dream; Oz was approached by Victoria and she told him that the man named Bishop Elbert and his religious comrades were involved in a child pornography ring and became informed that the ring is under investigation and about to be exposed. The four have been holding five young missing boys captive and using them not only for pornography, but as sex mates for more than a year.

Bishop Elbert, the ring leader and mastermind of the on-going sex and porno ring, according to Victoria, got first word of a man by the name of Jordan Mitchell who had been actively exposing violent child predators in the Chicago area and seemingly always around or implicated when the body of a known child murderer turned up. Bishop Elbert and his group were aware of the larger number of child sex abusers that were turning up missing or dead and recently had lost one of their own associates to a train accident that was reported by the police as suspicious. The suspicious part was Jordan Mitchell, known in the dream world as Xe. Xe was an angel just like Oz, Ehsa, Ber, Clay and Jax. He was the angel that possessed Jordan's body while he was in his deepest sleep pattern. Xe was stronger than Oz when it came to the vengeance of murdered children. He was an avenger without mercy and wasted no time putting the molesters to sleep permanently.

Xe was supposedly onto the Bishop's roll in the use and abuse of young boys. The bishop used his power in the Catholic Church to identify and lower boys into sexually vulnerable positions by first convincing them that they were gay and then threatening them by making them aware that their sexual tendencies would be acceptable as long as they were performing and being forgiven in the name of Jesus Christ our Lord. Subsequently they became very easy to manipulate for the personal pleasures of a certain Cardinal that knew how to mold and groom young boys into willing participants. Bishop Elbert and his flock panicked and made the decision to eliminate the threat of being uncovered by ridding themselves of the captive boys and any evidence that existed. They did so by sedating and burning them alive in a storage pod and placing it at the bottom of Lake Michigan. The four holy men completed their deadly task and swore to each other that they would never divulge this horrifying sin to anyone other than God.

Shortly after what Victoria said was a mass murder of the boys, Jordan Mitchell began having unbearable dreams of the five boys momentarily awaking in the storage pod in the bottom of a lake. He was told that they were placed there by a holy priest whom they'd learned to trust. When Jordan did fall into a deep enough sleep to unleash Xe he was so angry that he immediately went to confront Bishop Elbert. Xe found himself in the rear room of a church somewhere north of Chicago and in the presence of four men that thought of themselves as gods and thought of Xe as a fallen angel attempting to do the work of satin. They had no intention of permitting Xe to interfere with those that work in the name of God. Xe asked the question,

"By what right and whose guidance have you men taken away the happiness and lives of those babies?"

"Who are you?" asked the Bishop

"I'm Xe and I've come from the hearts and souls of the children that you have violated. I asked again; what gave you the right to violate theses five children?"

"The young boys were presented to us to make them whole again in the name of Jesus. They were distraught unloved and without Christ in their lives. We brought them to Jesus to be whole again with the word of God" answered the Bishop. Xe was so infuriated that his posture swelled like a weight lifter flexing every muscle in his body and face, again he asked.

"What and who exactly gave you the right to violate them?"

"They had no reason to live; they were abandoned by their mothers and society. No one wanted them; we took them in. We fed, clothed, and treated them with affection. It was they who yearned for sexual fondling in their own neglected spirits. They yearned to be caressed and to experience the loving touch of someone who cared. We gave them love and understanding even when our hearts were against it. We made ourselves vulnerable to sinful ways because of our desire to please and give them something to live for. They did not wish to go back to the life from where they had come. They desired and expressed their readiness to enter into the arms of Christ our Lord."

"Liars! You are all devious malicious liars for whom hell holds a special place," said Xe.

"Who are you to judge us? We are servants of God and have dedicated our lives to saving souls and sacrificing life's simple pleasures to comfort others. These children were blessed to have been able to return some of the pleasures that we have given to so many."

"I'll tell you who I am; I am Xe, a small remnant of the will of God himself is within me. A good and courage's man is within me and the will of the messengers of God have stirred my heart against the ways of child molesters and rapist. I have been angered by the spirits of these five children and intend to avenge their murders. Now I'm here before you; how do you choose to pay for your unforgivable infractions? That's my question to you, you, you and you. How do you choose to satisfy their demand for vengeance?"

"We have asked and have been forgiven by the Lord for our yielding and wayward discretions. We will continue on doing the ever so important work of God and the church. We have taken a vow not to let the devil control the lust that has been implanted in us as vulnerable human beings. We have change our ways to give us the strength to push away the temptations of satin and his lustful attack upon us and those sacrificial lambs. We are moving ahead for the betterment of the church".

"No!" said Xe. "You shall not move ahead from this room. On this day you shall pay in full for the lives that you have taken. The lives that never began and the lives that will never know what might have been. It is here and now that their wishes of vengeance should be satisfied." With that statement still upon his lips Xe grabbed the throat of the man of God standing closes to him.

With his might he lifted him off of the floor in attempt to choke off his wind. Without warning the Bishop standing behind him pulled a dagger from his cloak and plunged it into the back of Xe. Again and again he stabbed, for Xe had forgotten that he was now only a man with the heart and spirit of the angel that he once was. Xe released his grip from the holy man's neck as he started to become faint and without strength. As he began to collapse to the floor Jordan Mitchell awaken to find him truly dying in his own nightmare. The four priests were standing over him as those he had never seen before. He asked,

"What has happened to me?"

"You sacrificed your life for the lives of others."

"Where are the children?" he asked.

"They are awaiting you to let you know you have failed. There is no excuse for failure Mr. Mitchell. Now let us live in peace."

"The others will succeed I will make it so"

"There are no others, just you and you have failed …"

"Failed?" Jason was awakened by the horrifying end to a hero's life. A hero named Jordan Mitchell and an angle named Xe. Jason stood up and walked over and pulled the shades of the patio window open. He was hurting inside. This was not one of his typical dreams where the bad guy died; this was a dream that brought on the death of a good man. Though Jason had never heard of him or the angel, Oz had, during the brief encounter in Youngstown making the sting of his death feel like that of a long time friend. He was glad he had awakened. He was glad it was just a dream. His mind raced repeatedly back to the stabbing of Jordan by the priest as he gazed out of the glass at his favorite view.

"What's wrong dear?" came the voice of Helen, "have you had another nightmare?" she questioned in a sorrowful tone of voice. "Come here, let me hold you." Jason got into bed with a troubled look upon his face and a certain concern of emptiness with-in.

"I've had another nightmare that's true, but in this one the cry came from a man and an angel. It seems that their lives have been taken by a man of God."

"Were they evil men who deserved to die? Helen asked. "No, the man and the angel were one, they, or rather he, was a good man that deserved to live forever. I hope the dream stems from the guilty feeling that I sometimes have about Oz's actions. I hope this was a dream without meaning or reality." Jason was silent for a few moments leaving an opening for the question of his mate.

"None of your dreams are meaningless lately. Why should this be any different? Was Oz in your dream?"

"No, but there was an angel name Xe, he carelessly under estimated the vulnerability of his human factor and in my dream he was stabbed in the back multiple times."

"That's frightening to me; maybe there is a message in this dream that Oz can carelessly get you killed to honey. Oh my God, that's so frightening," she repeated. "Maybe it's time for you and Oz to let the law handle the pedophiles that you and he despise so greatly. Maybe this is a warning dream for you from them."

With Helen still talking the phone rang, it was Ben he sounded distraught and paused a lot between words.

"Jason … I've got to tell you about my dream! This morning I woke up knowing a good man had been murdered." Jason remained silent as Ben continued. "He was on a dream mission to avenge the lives of five young boys that had been held captive and used for sexual activates by many men. The night angel of the man was confronted by these five men and caught off guard and stabbed to death while he attempted to avenge the death of five children that they conspired to murder.

"I was awakened by the face of the good man wearing a wearing a look of 'how could this happen?' upon his face as he died. He seemed to demand that I come to him and avenge his death and the deaths of the children. This dream was the first I ever had that the angel involved was not Ehsa. I don't believe my dream angel is aware of my nightmare. I don't think the dream went far enough to awaken him. What do you make of that?" Ben asked Jason.

"Well that is a disturbing development, let me call you back in a few minutes" asked Jason. Jason hung up the phone giving Helen a sense that something or some problem just grew bigger.

"Come on, tell me what's going on now," she asked.

"Ben had the same dream that I had; I'm going to call the others to see if they too have had this nightmare. Something is brewing and I can feel it and its not coming to me through Oz. I don't believe he knows what has happened." With that he proceeded to call and confirm that Ben's dream had been the dream of the four men that Jason knew were actively taking the law into their own hands during their sleeping hours. Once confirmed, he called Ben.

"Benjamin, I think we have a serious problem. The dream that you told me you had this morning … We all had the same dream without the involvement of our counterparts. I guess the question is how can we find out if it has any truths?" "Well I can follow up on the name of the Bishop in my dream, he was clearly named Bishop Elbert something or another. I doubt that there is more than one Bishop Elbert something. I guess it wouldn't do any good to follow up on missing or exploited children since the dream indicated that they had been captive and secrets for quite some time. I can check and see if there is a Jordan Mitchell that fit the description of an active child protective advocate. That should be easy, and I can check and see if a body of a man has turned up over the last couple of days that fits Jordan's description once we have one" stated Ben.

"That sounds good, oh and remember the Church or Monetary is somewhere in North Chicago and I'm pretty sure it was happening during our dreams. That means the body may still be there, or at least there might be some blood evidence of a murder."

Jason said, "I'll do my part here but I think we should go up there on our own to look for the facts inconspicuously."

"I agree," Ben said.

"I'll get Helen to book us two flights to Chicago today."

"Good deal; lets role with it," Said Ben.

Jason called to informed Mack, Charles and Rocko of his and Ben's intentions. Without hesitation they each responded by saying.

"I'll see you in Chicago tomorrow" without hesitation all five men were headed to Chicago on behalf of their own person.

"Ok we'll all meet at the O'Hara Airport tomorrow at 6p.m.," Jason said.

†

More than half of all convicted sex offenders are sent back to prison within a year. Within 2 years, 77.9% are back.

— California Department of Corrections

†

Like rape, child molestation is one of the most unreported crimes: only 1 of 10 are ever disclosed

— FBI Law Enforcement Bulletin

†

The behavior is highly repetitive, to the point of compulsion, rather than resulting from lack of judgment.

— Dr. Ann Burges, Dr. Nicholas Groth, et al. in a study of imprisoned offenders

CHAPTER SEVEN

In the mean time Ben was in the police department data bank gathering all of the available information on Bishop Earl McBride and his holly men, several issues stood out. Many children had been reported missing in the area. They have vanished without a clue.

The Catholic Church in that area was one of the most prominent in the country. It had a vast congregation with social and political connections matching that of the Vatican. The area under Bishop Elbert's control was known for its popularity among priest due to its being a large center for orphaned and unwanted children.

Ben's concern was, why it was so popular among priests and why it always, according to intensive police documents, had been a focal point for missing and exploited children. Ben noted that more than twenty years ago skeletal remains of ten small children were found during a construction project. In addition there were remains of newborns that sent a brief shockwave across the nation.

With the limited amount of information gathered, Ben was still mostly concerned about the sexual and porno activity portrayed in his dream that led to the murderer of five young boys and the self-proclaimed angel of the abused children. In the meantime, Jason was doing some quick investigation on his own. He discovered that that particular area in Chicago had one of the highest numbers of missing and exploited children in the state with a foot note of (never being recovered; the highest in the entire country.)

On December 14th five good men came together at Chicago O'Hara airport terminal. None of them were sure of exactly why they were so bent on getting there but they all knew that being there was a part of their uncontrolled destiny. Jason took a minute to re-introduce everyone and to briefly explain why he thought that these five good men had encountered this frightening reality. "Once confirmed I'm not sure what exactly we will or should do. Three of you are police detectives that alone should assist us in making the right decisions. Charles and I are businessmen with a compassionate concern for children. Together I believe we are headed for the challenge of our lives. Based on the unconfirmed lost of the life of our dream comrade Jordan, we are all here in a city none of us have ever been. I guess you could say we are all chasing the same dream or should I say nightmare," Mack spoke in his conservative educated way.

"I believe we're here to answer the questions of five children that were violated and have had their lives shortened by an evil force dressed as a priest.

All of you here are aware of the cruelty that lies in the spirits of some men. Some are never awakened to the lustful spirits than can stir up fear and devastation in the lives of innocent babies. I think we've all been blessed and yet cursed to be able to hear their cries. The question becomes what should we do about it? Should we turn our heads and enjoy the safety of our own somewhat sheltered lives or should we strap on our armor and bring our chivalry into exis-tence as a joint force against a foe that is well inner woven within our society. I say let's do what we have done all of our lives instinctively, let's take away their cloak and put them where they belong. What do you think Charles?"

Charles looked around in his intelligently courteous way.

"Well I'll say this; I think I know why I'm here. I too feel the urging to bring this disease to an end. At the same time I know that we may be approaching a foe that's connected to the roots of man kind's own self destructive creation. We can't afford to under estimate what we are up against. If we do, we may all end up like our fallen friend before we get started"

"Your turn, Rocko," Jason said.

"You know what I say as an ex-army ranger turned detective. There are two things I have on my mind, we must know our enemy and we cannot under estimate their strength. Exposing them is a baby step. I personally think we should take them to justice like Malcolm X once said, 'by any means necessary'. If the way gets tuff you can count on me to have your back."

"Ben, I guess we're back to you. What's the plan?" asked Jason.

"If you read between the lines of all the information we've gathered, not just this case but all of the events of the past year. You'll find a lot of roughness at the bottom of this shit pile. I believe these folks are at the bottom of an effort to permit the use of children in any way that they choose. Like Jason, I say they do it as a challenge to temp God pertaining to commandments unsaid.

I agree with everything you all have said. I say we take the bull by the horn with the element of surprise. Let's follow our dream and expose the nightmare to the world," Ben said.

"There's nothing left for me to say," said Jason. "Here we are five good men in the city of Chicago on a mission that was given to us in our sleep. I guess the subliminal question is what do we intend on doing. Have we come to expose a crime or commit a crime? I'm not sure of the answer. So … first things first, let's get some rest and head for the church first thing in the morning."

"Do you think we can all make it through the night without our better halves taking things into their own hands?" asked Charles.

"That's a good question, I don't know. None of us seem to have any control over what we do once we are asleep. For the sake of Bishop Elbert and his flock I hope Oz and company can be contained," said Jason.

We'll meet in the lobby for breakfast at 6: am and we'll get to it, hopefully we won't be too late.

In the morning all five men were present and ready to go.

"Did anyone have a nightmare of any sort?" asked Jason.

"No, just a faint voice from Victoria urging each of us to act on behalf of the five murdered boys." Someone answered and continued. "Doesn't anyone else think it's strange that all of our dreams remained limited to Victoria's encouragement and nothing from the dead boys?"

Jason answered, "Yes, I too thought last night would be a night that Oz and the others would be taken to their limits. I guess we wanted them to do our dirty work so we could all just go home safely to our families. It doesn't appear that anything happened. Okay Ben what's the plan?"

"Well first we've got to find the place where Jordan was murdered. I have an address; strangely after asking where it's located I've found that it's nearly a two-hour drive just north of Chicago. I'm told that the place has actually been abandoned for a couple of years. I got a car waiting for us out front and a print out of the exact location," said Ben.

"I guess my question is still, what are we going to do when we get there, asked Mack. "Do we have a plan from the point of arrival?"

Jason responded, "Well I guess we're going to look for some indication that a murder was committed and seek the body of Jordan Mitchell. And if the evidence is obvious; we can call the authorities.

"Do you think the body would still be there after three days," asked Roco.

"I don't know but I'm sure we can convince the clergy men, if they are still there, to come clean with a little bit bully tactics of our own.

They headed northwest with Charles driving the rented Yukon nine passengers SUV. All five men were prepared for the cold, the snow and the winds blowing off of Lake Michigan. As they drove along the highway the visibility kept them from going anywhere near the speed limit. There wasn't much conversation, just five solemn faces. Each mind wondered from the good things of their past to the task at hand.

No matter how brave a man might be most men are intelligent enough to give fear ample space to cause concern and caution. These men aren't most men; fear had no place to dwell in any of their hearts. There is an old saying born of the biblical philosophy; it goes something like this; "where good men dwell evil has no place." These were not only good men; these men are compassionate, brave and unselfish. Jason broke the silence.

"I got a question for everybody; why are we here? Its freezing cold snowing like hell and we're on a mission based upon a dream, going to a place none of us has been. Hell none of us even has a weapon!"

"I do," said Ben as he showed his gloc-9.

"I do," said Rocko pulling out his nine mm.

"Me, too," said Charles showing his .44 magnum.

There was a long pause before Mack said, "I've got my police revolver. I just went from thinking I was the only one smart enough to bring a weapon to realizing now that I'm out gunned."

"Well", said Jason after a pause. "I'm the only one who brought just a cell phone, flashlight and a compass. I guess I'll be able to see my compass at night and call you guys if there's trouble." That statement brought a burst of laughter.

"Here" said Ben you can use my pocket knife" that brought another round of laughter.

"Ha, ha, ha," said Jason sarcastically. "I'm not even going to ask how all of you got those weapons past airport security"

"Yeah, don't ask," said Roco.

"Are we going up there to kill someone?" asked Jason.

"No," replied Ben. "We're going up there with artillery so we won't be killed."

They drove another sixty or so miles before Roco broke the silence again.

"Hey did you guys ever hear what happened to the security guard at the Homewood cemetery? There's a story going around that on a hot July evening a guy was driving his route and checking for vandals.

"Anyway, he drove along the Homewood side of the cemetery without seeing anyone. It had just gotten dark and he thought that he heard music. He turned off the air conditioner and rolled down the window to listen for its source. And sure enough someone was playing the wedding march as loud as their speakers would allow.

"He slammed on his breaks and jumped out of the car only to find himself alone and no one in sight and not a sound. He looked around the concrete mausoleums and the six and seven foot head stones that are in the right hand section of the cemetery. Seeing that he was the only living person in the cemetery he got back in his car and continued his route.

"After the long winding drive he ended back where he had heard the wedding music. Lying in the middle of the street in front of him he spotted a bridal bonnet. He got out and picked it up and used his flashlight to look around because by now it was pitch back outside.

"Of course it was night and there was no one there. He jumped back into his car and headed back on his patrol after throwing the bonnet out onto the roadway. He suddenly slammed on breaks again after looking into the rearview mirror and spotting a woman in a wedding dress bent over and picking up the bonnet. He looked back over his shoulder and it was still pitch black and no one in sight.

He then looked through the dash board mirror and saw what appeared to be hundreds of people all in wedding celebration garb celebrating and cheering on the bride and groom to the loud music. Seeing enough he jumped out of the car again only to find that there was no one there but him. Puzzled and apprehensive he slowly got back into the car looking around into the darkness with his flashlight. He started to drive off and the music started to blast again.

Through his rear view mirror was the vision of many well-dressed people dancing in the roadway behind him. Ahead it was still pitch black and in the mirror a celebration. He stomped on the gas pedal getting away causing them to become smaller and smaller and the music went from loud to faint as he exited the graveyard. When he told me the story he swore to me that it was true. I asked him what he made of the grave yard wedding; he said he thinks that dead people celebrate a life that we can't know about and the rear view mirror strangely let him see what others could not."

"So, what did he do?" asked Mack

"He quit the job, he said he didn't want to see the dead celebrating like the living and he said he was scared to return."

"That sounds ridiculous," said Ben

"Who are we to talk, we're the ones that thought last night's dreams bring to life to the likes of Oz and Xe to take our bodies and do what we can't get angry enough to do ourselves. No one really knows the ways and means of communication between the dead and the living. Whether it is a rear view mirror or a deep sleep I think the dead have ways of getting their message to us if we have enough concern to listen," said Mack.

"Shut up man, you're scaring me. We have enough mystery in our lives already. We can't afford to try and figure this all out," said Roco.

"He's right; no more scary stories. We've got to stay focused. We may be in real danger and were less than an hour from the men that kill babies," said Ben.

"I, for one, have got to stay on top of the ruthless things that men can do. We can't tamper with things in the spiritual realm but we can look a child molester in the eyes and take away their ability to make pedophilia a common occurrence in our communities. As far as the Oz's and the Xe's we release, remember they are still us and we remain them. Jordan Mitchell proved that we live and die as one. They're just us in our subliminal mood of merciless revenge for the death of the innocent. Oz is me and I am Oz on this mission I hope we can remain in one of the same. I need to stay angry and unforgiving and I'm sure you guys feel the same way too. There are five of us in this car not ten. That story may reflect us in the sense that we have two visions. We have the ability to dream and see what happened to those that would otherwise have just vanished at the hands of evil men. I have a second vision that we may somehow learn to prevent or at least make men aware of the boundaries set by the good within us all. Let's tell them to leave the children alone," said Jason.

"Amen to that, lets kick ass and send the message," said Rocko.

"Amen" one voice.

"I've never seen this much snow on a highway in my life. What are we going now, about 10 miles per hour?" asked Charles.

"Right about now I wish we were going 10miles per hour, the navigator hasn't spoken since we got off the main highway, I hope we're going the right way. The snow is so thick I can't see more than twenty feet. Ten minutes ago there was a truck in front giving me lights to follow. He pulled over a while back and I haven't seen another vehicle in either direction. There are no tracks to follow, just the guard rails, if you want to call the metal ropes guard rails."

"Just take your time, we'll get there and we will have a better element of surprise because I know they don't expect any visitors on a night like this," said Ben "Look there's a sign, it say's St John's Parish one mile. Is that what we're looking for? It looks like a very old sign," Said Rocco.

"What are you doing? Why are we stopping?" asked Jason.

"I've got to make sure I'm in four wheel drive, all there is, is snow up to the head lights and the only reason I know I'm on a road at all is the line of evergreen trees off to our right."

"This vehicle is always in four wheel drive so you might as well keep driving," Said Ben.

"I guess you'll just have to follow the flatness of the snow with the road under it.

"I'm trying; this is like driving in the dark, I'm glad there are no hills up here in no man's land. We're barely moving without spinning the wheels."

"Just keep it up, you're doing just fine," Said Ben after another twenty minutes of creeping along in the two or three feet of snow. The next voice was that of the driver.

"Damn it!" Charles said as the car went crashing through what appeared to be a fence crossing the street in front of him.

"I think we've just gone through a fence or gate, now we're spin- ning tire and not going anywhere I think we're stuck."

"Okay, stop. Let me get out so I can see what's going on," said Jason. He and Ben got out of the car with Rocko and Mack right behind.

"I can't see shit," Ben said.

"There's no shit to see," Rocko responded.

"I guess we'll have to sit here and wait for morning when we can see where we're at," said Ben.

"Wait this isn't a gate we've hit it's a rail of a drive way. Look at the huge dark spot looming in front of us. It's a building, I think we're here," Said Jason.

"I'll be damn. We are here, let's first see if there's anyone else here before we make any more noise. So much for the element of surprise," said Ben.

By now everyone was standing outside of the car gawking up at the huge complex that was sitting about a hundred yards in front of them in the darkness with no sign of life. The snow of course con- tinued to dump upon everything in sight. They stood for a moment looking around in every direction and listening for a sound of any kind.

"Well … what are we going to do, we can't stand here all night," said Ben. Rocko got something from the car and started walking.

"I guess that means let's go," said Mack as everyone else grabbed a few things and headed toward the building. After about ten min- utes they stepped into a covered exterior entryway. Looking into darkness of the windows they searched around what appeared to be a huge porch of some sort.

"Well at least we're out of the snow," Ben said and grabbed and rattled the eight-foot high double entry doors. "We're locked out and guess what, there's a pad lock on the outside and no one seems to be here for us to surprise."

"Well that means that we're welcome to go in … kick it in Rock," Jason said. One hard kick and the doors were open and swinging on their hinges.

Using their flashlights they explored every direction in the huge hotel lobby type foyer. There were two staircases leading to upper floors on either side of the room. At the rear between the two staircases there were two more double doors. Rocko and Ben had already opened and entered the adjacent rooms with the flashlights bouncing all around the walls and ceilings and the other three men were right behind them.

"Well," Ben said, "it looks like we are truly alone."

Jason and Charles were clicking light switches and opening side doors that seemed to lead to smaller walkways.

"Nobody leave this room, we've got to stay together until we know for sure that there is know no danger," said Jason.

"There's a fire place … lets burn some of this old furniture and get a fire going. We can melt some snow for water, and we can find the kitchen and see if there's anything to eat. First thing in the morning we can check the place out better and see what we need for the car. I don't know about you guys, but I have no phone service. I hope it's because of the winter storm and not that we're in a no service area."

†

*Because convicted sex offenders and molesters may already have a prior record, and because the risk for re-arrest is high among sex offenders, many judges impose a special sentencing for those convicted. Some convicted sex offenders and molesters might be ordered to go into psychiatric treatment or a sex offender's treatment program

†

*According to the survey of Inmates of State Correctional Facilities, the judge ordered approximately 13% of the child victimizers into treatment programs. 29% of convicted molesters who are already confined for forcible sodomy of a child were also ordered into a treatment program.

†

* Of those released sex offenders who were accused of another sex crime, 40% were arrested for a new offense within a year after their release.

†

"No question; I've got grandchildren of my own and I know what I would do if someone touched them … they can kiss it goodbye. We need to let them know that there is no punishment great enough."

— Anthony Jones,
Washington D.C. businessman

CHAPTER EIGHT

The night crept by slowly with everyone quiet but no one sleeping. The building may have been empty but it made all kinds of strange noises as the wind howled throughout the night. Jason stirred after what seemed like a brief moment of sleep. He slowly opened his eyes, Ben and Rocko was standing above him with their eyes as red as fire.

"Oz, we need to talk. Clay feels that we shouldn't be here and Ber and Jax concur. We respect your judgment; however we feel that we have not been summoned by the spirits of children but instead a voice of deception. The motive of being here is suiting for the human side of our being but not strong enough to awaken us. According to our human dreams one of us has been put to death along with our mortal body. We are confused, not by the fact that we're inseparable from our human counterpart, but by the fact that he was an angel and was so un-expecting of their capability to killing him. It seems like an easy kill that has make it seem like we, too, are easy prey for an evil predator.

"We are concerned that if conflict does occur here it will be between evil and the five humans that we have had the honor of sharing their bodies made of substance. We may all be dead by morning or without a vessel from spirit to mass. And lastly, this place smells of an evil of a different kind. Our human sides, as brave and courageous as they are, are no match for those that are destined to serve themselves as gods and will preserve their rights to commit and justify their acts of mayhem.

"You know as well as I do that these monsters need to be dealt with without compassion. Our human counter parts are burdened with a desire to be forgiving and understanding on issues that they cannot begin to comprehend. How can we rest assured that we will be the ones that confront God's adversary," asked Ehsa. Jason though drowsy yielded to himself as Oz in need to answer as an angel.

"You are correct we could all be in jeopardy with this well meaning journey of five brave men. I too have sensed something very wrong here, however we must respect their efforts of courageous good men on a mission that has obviously been inspired by our activities during their sleeping hours. You know as well as I that without them we have no conduit or ability to respond to the cries of these or any innocent victims. I concur that these types of men are as rare as the voice of God. Before them I didn't know where we dwelt. I was limited to containing my anger without an outlet; with them I've been able to act as our creator intended. Until we can act separate from them on our own I'm afraid we must simply hope that they are wise enough to unleash their inner self when in danger. They obviously cannot use us at will, nor can we utilize their mass when we choose. Something is very wrong here that we're not privileged to. Jason is going to be in control of his inner self and taken it upon himself and his mortal comrades to stand up for the causes of all of us. I knew Xe as an angel of spirit since the conduit is dead I'm not sure that he still exist. We rely upon their dreams to be awakened and even then we are not aware of each other's works until they communicate with each other. This man Jordan Mitchell had no communication with Jason. Jason was obviously unaware that he existed until the dream of his murder by a pedophile Bishop and then at the word of Victoria and not the child victims, which in itself is puzzling. There were no cries from the children. We have not been able to respond to the devious acts but all have taken it upon themselves to investigate. I don't know what they intend to do but they all seem to be well armed. All we can do is hope they have thought their actions through and not end up like Jordan Mitchell. I wish we knew the enemy, let's look around before they awaken, though it will do no good."

"Eight a.m.!" Rocko shouted, "Everybody wake up! I've been looking around and have found a couple of things that are interesting to say the least."

After the ordinary stretching and the yawning the four men followed Rocko up a center stairwell to the very top of an old bell tower over looking the complex. One at a time they reach the top of the snow covered observation platform. There was a magnificent view of the wintery landscape for miles without a structure in site. They stood silently gazing out at the winter wonderland it was incredibly beautiful. *How could a place so mesmerizing be chosen to commit such evil acts?* Just below them lay the roof of the building. The building was shaped like the letter T with the entry corridor located beneath them at the center. After hours of prowling around in the every room they concurred that the room in the dream was not there. Just before giving up the search Rocko's military voice boomed out again.

"Hey … take a look at this." At the bottom of the staircase leading to the upper bell tower there was an iron door lying under a thick dirty floor covering behind the starting point of steps. When they opened up the two trap doors they discovered another staircase going downward and there was evidence that it had been recently used. After a few turns downward it became pitch black.

"We've got to go back up and get the flashlights and there's a gas lantern out in the truck," Jason said. They retreated and got the flashlights and waited for Mack to come back from the SUV with the lantern. After about twenty minutes. Ben and Rocko went out to see what had happened to Mack or why was he taking so long to return. In the nearly waist deep snow they followed his tracks. They finally caught up with Mack he was standing along the end of the driveway railing with his back to them. He turned around slowly once they called out his name.

"Mack what's up? I didn't realize we had walked such a long way last night," said Ben.

"It's not here." The truck is not here, I know this is where we left it. You can see that new snow has covered the indentation where we went off the road and crashed into the fence. I have the keys right here in my hand. It looks like it was backed out of and driven away the same direction that we came. I don't see tracks of a second vehicle that may have brought someone here. But what I do see," He said while pointing back toward the complex, "is that there are two sets of foot prints other than ours coming this way. I think they came from the building and drove off in our truck last night."

"Lets go back and inform the others and plan away to get away from here today," said Ben. The three men headed back to the complex meeting Jason and Charles on the way.

"Where have you guys been? We became a little worried and headed this way," said Jason.

"Something strange is going on. The SUV is gone and by the amount of snow lying in the area, it's been gone since last night. And…who ever took it appeared to have walked from here while we were sleeping. I did notice that beneath the newly fallen snow there appeared to have been a scuffle of some sort," said Mack.

"Let's get back out of the cold and do whatever it will take to get us out 'a here," said Jason.

"Yeah, well first lets go see what's down the staircase, it's the only place we didn't explore," said Rocko.

As soon as they got inside they headed for the stairwell and proceeded downward four flights of steps. At the bottom of the steps was a corridor lined with small holding cells. They proceeded slowly shinning the flashlight in each cell as they moved along. At the end of the corridor were two huge metal doors that were wide open. They entered the room, which was empty, but it led to another room just ahead. At the second set of doors they shined in their lights before entering.

"This is it; this is the room of the dreams. I know this is it, I can smell the evil," said Rocko.

"I agree," said Jason. "This is it."

Everyone agreed that they were at the scene of many crimes mainly the killing of Jordan. The room was huge and had more than twenty white beds equipped with straps across the middle. They were ruffled and they all appeared to have been slept in. As they were shinning their lights all around the ceiling room lights came on lighting up the room with florescent lights. Mack had located a throw switch and tried it and it worked.

"Voilà," he said jokingly as if he knew what he was doing. "It worked. So what more do you want" he said while shrugging his shoulders. "I'm good at what I do."

"Quit clowning, lets find some evidence of what happened to Jordan in here," said Ben. "Everybody look around for dried blood or a sign of a struggle. Anything we can use to take to the police is what we're looking for."

After nearly an hour of looking around, all five men concluded that there was nothing there. There was a round table in the center of the room under one of the light fixtures. They all sat down, facing each other, as Jason spoke, "I'm not feeling anything; I expected to find a bloody room and a lot of untouched proof of what the Bishop did."

"Me too, but it's not to be. It seems that nothing at all happened here," said Ben "Listen!" Rocko said as he got up and ran to the light switch.

"Listen to what?" Jason asked.

"Shhhhh," everyone seemed to respond at the same time.

"I don't hear anything," Jason said in a whisper just as Rocko killed the lights. In a few seconds it was obvious that someone was coming through the outer doors. As they came forward with flashlights moving around the room, Rocko clicked on the lights just as the five men, one dressed in the clothing of a priest, stumbled into the middle of the room. Within a split second they found themselves surrounded by five armed men including Jason. In defense of what they thought was an ambush. Jason and company were spread out in the room and had the upper hand.

"Put your guns on the floor or die!" Ben said in a strong voice of authority. "Put'm down now!"

With all the weapons pointed at their heads they slowly lowered their weapons to the floor!

"Who are you" Jason asked.

"I'm Bishop Evans and these are my friends. What are you doing here?" The Bishop asked while holding his hands up high.

"I'll ask the questions; what are you doing here?" asked Jason.

"Well it may sound strange, but we're here because we got wind that some pedophiles were in the act of harming a group of children" answered the Bishop, and this is were it was happening."

"Who told you this?" asked Jason.

"Well again, it may sound strange but we are actually responding to all of our similar but realistic dreams."

"Cut with the bullshit Rev!" Where's Jordan Mitchell's body?" Ben asked, as he moved his weapon to the head of Bishop.

"Speak now or I'll take you out' a here right on the spot."

"Wait! Wait! Jordan is not dead; he's standing here next to me."

"I'm Jordan," said the man standing next to the Bishop.

"What" Ben said, "you're telling a lie. I'm not going to ask you again."

"This time speak up and save your life idiot," Rocko said, as four of the five men redirected their guns to the head of the man claiming to be Jordan Mitchell. "Wait!" said the Bishop, "don't shoot, we are who we say we are and we've killed no one. We're here to save the children," he said. "Unless you are all murdering pedophiles we're not here to do you any harm."

"Explain yourself," Ben demanded without lowering his weapon.

"You will find it hard to believe but, we have all been cursed with late night dreams or spiritual messages from children that have been murdered by cold blooded child rapist. I've been active here in Chicago for years trying to bring awareness to families about pedophilia and child abuse. I've had the pleasure of meeting these four young men while on my quest to stomp out the evil ways that are leading to an outbreak of many deplorable abuses inside of homes, and our catholic church. Jordan is one of the men that was accused of confronting and killing a known child rapist down in Gary, Indiana, a few months ago. He wasn't aware that he had killed the murderer during a scuffle with him until he woke up the next morning with blood soaked clothing and a slight memory of being at the crime scene. After talking to him later I found that he, like the rest of us, had been involved in late night attacks on child molesters during his deepest hour of sleep. We all began to talk at one time or another, discovering that we have been taking the law into our own hands during a particular stage of sleep. It's been going on for more than a year. This past week we all concurred that we were having the same dream concerning five young boys that were being sexually molested by my fellow priest and that they may have been put to death to cover up the infractions that occurred right here in this room."

"The child in you dream, was her name Victoria?" asked Jason

"No" answered the Bishop, "it was a little boy named Victor who had been in all of our dreams at one time or another prior to now. I know it's all so hard to believe but I swear to you that it's true."

Ben and the crew began to ease up as they realized that the five men that they surrounded were here due to a dream similar to theirs.

"This victor in your dreams, how did he get you to come here?"

"He told us in the dream that four of the catholic priest involved had been uncovered by a man named Rocco Boyd who had been ambushed by the priest and was murdered here to protect their circle of pedophiles, and the church from being exposed. Jason and Ben glanced at each other and at the others that had come with them. This story sounded very much like their reason for being here.

"So how'd you end up here and why?" asked Jason.

"We came to seek proof of this man Rocco's killing and to see if we could perhaps save the lives of the five young boys," answered the Bishop. "We agreed that while we were awake and alert as men we may be able to bring these sick priest to justice rather than the swift vengeance of our counter parts during our sleep," answered the Bishop. Again Jason glanced around at his group of good men. Jason spoke out.

"Well it seems that all ten of us have been brought here for nearly the same reasons. This young man to my left is Rocco Boyd and as you can see, just like your Jordan, he is alive and well. And, it appears that nothing has occurred in this old perish or what ever it is, for years."

Ben whispered into Jason's ear, "Something is wrong with this picture."

"But if that's all true, why are we all here, what reason could be behind bringing the ten of us to an abandoned perish in the middle of nowhere?" the Bishop asked, while looking around at each man with his shoulders hunched. It dawned on everyone at about the same time that this must be some kind of trap. They all began to look around and slowly separate while backing toward the only entrance into the huge room. Suddenly the outer door slammed shut and the lights briefly flickered but came back on. They all instinctively ran towards the outer door colliding with it in full stride, but it did not budge.

"Someone has trapped us down here. Come on everybody push against the door at the same time." All of the men pushed against the six-foot wide huge metal enforced doors, to no avail. This sub floor was originally designed as a bomb shelter. It was a trap, but by whom? None of these men had any idea. After nearly an hour of attempting to push or pull the door down they had given up.

"Does anyone's cell phone work?" asked Ben.

"No" was the answer from every man in the room.

"This isn't good" said Ben.

"No," said Jason. "This is the worst than, not good, this is horrifying to say the least." Jason asked the Bishop if he knew of another way out.

"I haven't the slightest idea; I've never been in this building in my life."

"Okay let's not panic. We're all strong level headed men. Let's work to get out of this hell hole and God help whoever set us up like this," said Jason. Every man scurried around the entire basement level looking for away out, there was none and they were three stories below ground.

In less than an hour they began to except that they could be permanently trapped and that there was no way out. To make matters worst, hey had no way to contact anyone above ground for help. One at a time each man began to give up and sit down back in the inner room. For a short while there was nothing said and then the Bishop broke the silence.

"Well I guess now is a great time for prayer" The words hadn't completely left his lips when the overhead lighting began to flicker and ultimately shut off completely. The room was now pitch black. They couldn't even see their own hands when held up to their faces.

"I guess we might as well get some sleep, maybe someone will see our vehicle and come inside."

"Yeah, or maybe we're just ten good men about to meet our maker," said Mack. "You know I'm wondering what would happen if we do all fall asleep. I'm wondering if Oz or Ehsa would be capable of getting us out of this mess," Jason replied. "I have no way of knowing but it seems to me that Oz comes to life while I'm in a very deep sleep and only responds to the voice of a murdered child. It seems apparent now, but I assume that is the reason we are here instead of our counter parts. Our dreams did not summon Oz or any of the others because we responded to a voice of something or someone that had not been murdered; yet something that managed to cause our dreams to parallel each others and lead us to this entrapment. This is bigger than us men; this is spiritual in an evil way to rid us all at one time, said Jason.

"Your right" said the Bishop. This is a phenomenon that we as men cannot explain, it has no reasonable explanation and yet it has happened. I don't believe that going to sleep will help us. The dreams that brought on our subconscious supper men came at a point of sleep that took us into our own spiritual level that was obviously close to a level that we would not be able to awaken from.

I believe that our own hate for child murderers allowed us to go as close as we could go to descending into the next spiritual level that would mean no return. In other words, we came as close as we could get to dying in our sleep. It appears that we are doomed here to die just as someone or something has anticipated. We must have come too close to exposing a culture that has been here and hidden all over the world for many centuries."

"Are you saying that we were making an impact or ridding our world of a culture that thrives on child abuses?"

"Both, and yes, that's exactly what I'm saying. Think about it, or let me ask you, how many children have you avenged", asked the Bishop of Jason. Jason seemed to pause for the longest time before speaking out,

"I don't really know because I can't really clearly remember that I have taken any ones life. Yet, I would guess based upon the number of children that are no longer in my dreams that there may have been more than a hundred in the last year or so. I don't know that my thoughts on this can be true or not."

"There lies my point," said the Bishop. There are ten of us trapped below ground as a result of our own dreams. That could mean literally that we are responsible for the deaths of many evil men and just as we have a God to serve, so do they. Evil lurks very deep in the hearts of men. This evil blindness survives like any other disease that kills; it is evasive and cunning. Those men have justified their pedophilic ways by submitting to their desires while entering into spiritual wrong doing that offends God himself. Doing so, they have realized that they have hopelessly become the unforgivable and somehow molded together as a force that has justified its own reason for living. They have been cast away from God into an imaginary world of self-satisfying men without a God. Someone out there knows of our effort to eliminate them. They have learned to survive by using secrecy to perform their obsessions and to not be discovered. They've become beast and it has become a way of life for so many and we have become a threat to that way of life."

"This all sounds so unbelievable we are just men. I can't explain what has been happening during my sleep or why, but I find it hard to believe that we have been thrust into a realm of living that is meant for God's own", said Jason.

"Maybe we are God's way of putting a stop to the madness" said the Bishop. "Then why are we losing?" asked Mack.

"We haven't lost yet. What the Bishop said makes sense, how can we lose with God on our side?"

"Yeah, well how are the children dying with God on their side?"

"Maybe he's leaving it up to us," said Mack. "I've got an idea, let's try and think like ordinary men for a moment. Earlier I seen propane tank over near the examining table, maybe we can strap it onto the door some how and use our guns to causes it to explode. Maybe it will have enough force to blow a hole in it or something. We can use our cell phones as lights to guide us to the tank and outer door."

"You know what," said Ben, "he's right, I did see that a propane tank and I opened it a little, there was gas in it. We may blow ourselves up but it's worth a try."

"Let's do it" said Jason, "we are men, and we can't just sit here and die."

With the cell phone lights they located the propane tank and placed it on the floor at the middle of the outer doors.

"Wait!" said Mack. "It's not gonna work like that, we need to be sure it won't just explode and leave us trapped behind a fire. Let's pack the door with gun powder from our bullets, maybe it will add to the force of the explosion."

"There's got to be some fire extinguishers down here incase it does catch fire," said Ben. The extinguishers were quickly found near by. After Mack and Jordan packed the seams of the door with powder taken from their bullets they taped to the door with first aid tape. Ben closed the second set of doors and cracked it enough for his .44 magnum. With the propane tank slightly opened at the valve he took the shot. The flash and force pushed the men to the floor behind the second set of doors. They rushed to get up and regain themselves. With the door burning at the bottom and up the seam where the powder had been placed, Ben rushed through the smoke to extinguish the remaining flames.

"Is everybody all right?" Jason asked.

Once the fire was out they were back in the dark. The smoke had spread into the main room unseen. The lit embers in the area between the two doorways allowed some of the light into the adjacent room.

All eyes could faintly be seen as they all stayed locked on hot ember of the outer door that contained them. Ben and Jordan began to kick the door in the area of the explosion. Mack moved into the area with a piece of metal he had picked up and they stood aside as he stuck it into the widened crack between the doors. As he pried Jason came in with a longer piece of metal and several others braved the smoke to help with the leverage. The door gave a little below the center height down to the floor, but would not open enough for a man to slip through.

The Bishop continuously burned a piece of small twisted paper that he had lit with the embers. This provided a little more light. They took turns pounding and prying at the hole they had created. It was a little bigger than a baseball but growing a little at a time.

The door itself was made of three-inch hard wood clad by a sheet metal. The explosion dislodged the metal and caused it to separate from the wood for a few inches. Even though the hole was small, it was encouragement for the men to work feverishly and chip away at its size.

"Wait, we've got to take turns, we're getting in each others way with such a small area to work with. Jordan let a couple of the others work at it for a few minutes. I'm going further out into the room to see if I can find something bigger to pry with, but I need someone else's phone with a stronger light than mine. I'm leery of us using a flame for fear of burning us all up."

"Here use mine, it has the best light among what we have." Charles handed his phone to Ben. Several others went out into the darkness to seek something to work with. Jason walked over to Ben using his now dim cell phone light to see. "Hey, I hate to say this but we're losing oxygen. At this level it's probably due to our explosion among other things. I don't want to say anything and cause panic but, if we don't get out of here soon we really are going to go into a deeper sleep. "I know…and I'm sure that the rest of them are aware that all of our breathing is becoming more and more difficult," responded Ben. "You know what's kind of funny, none of us is smart enough to be afraid or we are just all extremely brave men without fear." While Jason was talking, the Bishop walked up to the two of them out of the dark.

†

9,700 convicted sex offenders were released in one year alone. Nearly 4,300 of the 9,700 were labeled child molesters. Approximately 70% of the victims were children

†

Nearly 50% of the of the victims were their own children or a relative

†

The average sentence given to the 4,300 convicted child molesters was approximately seven years, with three of the seven years typically being served

†

22% of the child offenders reported being sexually abused as a child

†

"After wrestling with the thought of a criminal that has committed a perverted act against a defenseless child it comes to mind to remove these people from society as we know it; never to have exposure to children again in any way shape or form.

It's hard to envision how our judicial system can communicate a proper punishment for such a heinous crime. The reason being; the child is destroyed mentally, emotionally and physically and there is no punishment that can restore the victim's state of being. People are different; some are much more treacherous than others; it's difficult to generalize a form of punishment that would be suitable in all scenarios. The justification should be administered in a case-by-case format. There will need to be an intricate evaluation of the perpetrator and the victim so that the appropriate punishment and the rehabilitation process can be applied."

— Charles Gaines

CHAPTER NINE

"Gentlemen," he said in a slurring voice, "we've got to get out of here soon or this will be come our tomb, four of the men that sat down to rest are sound asleep and starting to display a shortness of breath. After going to sleep and waking again, your friend Rocco is standing with red eyes and pounding and prying like there is no end to his energy. I believe he has transgressed to his angelic form."

"You're kidding me," said Ben. "Then again, maybe that's what we all need to do. I'm getting a little faint myself; I hope it's due to fatigue and not lack of oxygen. I'm going to have to sit down for a while."

Within a few minutes the only sound heard was Rocco's grunting and pounding at the bottom of the door with a medal bar of some kind.

"I think I've got it! Give me a hand on prying the whole door open, it's ready to give!" He said, while demonstrating that the door latch used to lock them in was hanging by a lose bracket. There was no help. They had all succumbed to lack of oxygen. Rocco roared, as the angelic side of all of their personalities often does while reaching inside themselves for the gifted strength. With his entire mite he gave one more crash into the door as it gave way and opened out into the stairwell going upward. The fully open door allowed air to pour down into the stair well from the cold air at the higher levels while the remaining smoke rose up. Once outside the room he pulled the electric lever that controlled the lights and discovered the nine others including Jason passed out but all were still alive. Two at a time he dragged them out into the naturally ventilated stairwell.

"Come on guys help me out here. Wake up and breath in some of this life." He dropped Ben to the floor and startled him into breathing and gasping for air while he went back into get Jason. He was laying about ten feet from the now beaten open door.

"Come on, big man, no sleeping on the job. We're not done yet." Jason, like Ben and the others, was not far from totally succumbing to the lack of breathable air. Once all nine bodies were out in the stairwell he sat down to rest as they all began to stir.

Jason's first sight was that of Rocco dragging one of the men out into the stairwell where he still sat on the cement floor attempting to gain back his strength. He drew his attention to Rocco's eyes; they were a glowing burnt orange. He knew that Rocco was not the Rocco that they all knew without a doubt he had been able to reach inside himself and release that inner self.

Jason momentarily wondered why none of the others were able to convert into or bring out the angel within. *Where is Oz?* he wondered.

He and the others recovered quickly and slowly made their way out of the lower floor dungeon and up onto the ground level of the building. With weapons drawn, they entered into the main entry area looking for who ever may have made the attempt to kill them. After a thorough search they found no one. There was no obvious sign that anyone else had been in the building. Everything they had left behind was sitting untouched right where they had left it. When they made their way outside they found the snow packed up against the huge entryway door with no foot prints or evidence that anyone had entered through the front. Their prints were covered by the snowfall that had accumulated throughout the day.

"Damn," Ben said. "There must be at least four feet of snow out here and there are no signs that anyone has left this building."

"There's our SUV down there to the left of that group of trees; well at least the roof of it from the doors up," the Bishop said as he pointed to the roof of the black SUV

"Is there any thing to eat in it?" One of the men asked

"I think there's some junk food that we bought at the gas station on the way here," the Bishop answered.

"Hey, my cell phone's working."

"Mine too." Nearly all of the men began dialing out to communicate with love ones. They had all came very close to death. Along with their desire to let someone know they were all right was the instinctive desire of good men; they were angry. Someone had attempted to kill them, they wanted to know who. As the phone conversations wound down they began to look again for clues of some sort. After a short time they gathered back into the main lobby where someone had built a fire using the pieces of furniture that was thrown about. Jason spoke "Well men I've noticed that everyone here is focused on the same thing, who done it? Does anyone have any ideas?"

"Well" Ben spoke out. "We came here looking for the Bishop and a band of pedophile priest and they came here looking for a group of child molesting men. Ironically we all came here for the same reason that is to rescue children and confront what we all thought to be an evil group of child murdering men. What we walked into was a trap to eliminate us. Apparently we were on to something that obviously has threatened their way of life. The question is, how they could have known all of us and how anyone could have the power to interfere with all of our dreams"

"Even though we've all been experiencing a kind of spiritual contact with deceased children, we are all men on a human mission to avenge and fight fire with fire. If someone has come to recognize these ten men as a threat; they are well organized and must have some access to a spiritual message just as we do. Who or what can be so concerned about the lives of child murderers that they would be bold enough to attempt to kill us all?" asked Jason.

"I think I know," responded the Bishop. "I'm ashamed to say it but, the only organization that has a lot to gain; and a lot to lose, is my own. Many priests and ministers have created their own flock of child predators. And … they have not only hidden their wickedness for centuries but they have learned from and taught each outer to justify their molesting activities. Now they are obviously obsessed with continuing their assault on those who are brave enough to stand up and put a stop to this madness.

"Please don't misunderstand me; most men of the cloth are clearly and without a doubt committed to the well being of the innocent and they are true to their vows to God and the church. But just like any other sector of men in our society there are those that are infected by mental and spiritual disorders that cause the acting out of selfish lust even to the point that it becomes habitual and dangerous to themselves and others around them. Neither the Pope nor God himself can alter the mind of a homicidal pedophile. They blind themselves to the act and justify it by pretending that it did not occur.

"In addition; through modern technology, they've learned to communicate with each other to encourage the acts as if it were acceptable because they are otherwise respected and honorable men. My understanding is that they now exchange morbid experiences even to the point of what they call disposing of their sacred cow.

"Now, here comes a group of men that are ordained by God, to put a stop to the abomination. However, we are men. We are vulnerable to the sting of death and they are aware of it. Our strength lies in our ability to interact with the spiritual good that lies within us. As you all know, while we're in our deepest sleep God's tools of vengeance are released into our human bodies. Between the ten of us we are responsible for the elimination of hundreds of addicted homicidal pedophile and we have probably saved the lives of thousands children.

"Obviously we are moving up the ladder to a hierarchy of a secret a society that is led by those that operate under a cloak of trust and godliness. How they know of us and we were not aware of each other is a mystery to me. I will not fall into such a trap again," said the Bishop.

"Ummm we have a bigger enemy than I thought," said Jason.

"Yeah," said Ben. "And I'd like to make our enemy a lot smaller in numbers. I'd like to do it while awake and without my God sent counter part."

"Without the dreams we may mistakenly harm the innocent. At least our dreams leave no doubt of the guilty; until now," said the Bishop. "Remember, we were set up by a supposed child victim named Victor or Victoria, that's been in our dreams all along."

"Well they've fooled us once let's not let it happen again," said Ben.

"I vote we let our sleeping avengers fight for us. They are stronger, smarter and more cunning than us … and their eyes glow enough to frighten any enemy. And I might add, they are a better match for the ruthlessness of child killers no matter who they are," said Jason.

"Amen to that," said one of the ten.

"Well let's get on our phones and get help getting out of here. I'm sure they know by now that their plan to eliminate us did not work. They must also know that Oz, Xe, Jax, Ehsa, Ber, Clay and Bishop's remaining four are stepping up the campaign to do God's will. I've got my money on us," said Jason.

"Let's get to work," said Ben. "I plan on sleeping as much as possible."

"I plan on taking a sleeping pill every night for the rest of my life until they are gone and babies are safe," said Jordan.

"Let's do it," said one of the men.

"Wait," said the Bishop. "I know it may sound silly to you all right now but we may never all see each other again until we are before God. Please let me say a prayer before we part.

"Good, that's good," said Ben. "Do it." All of the men nodded in agreement.

The Bishop was moved internally by his angel of vengeance as he bowed his head. "Lord God Almighty, we come to you as servants in every way. Please allow us as good men to remain strong enough at heart to act as your soldiers against the enemy of mothers all over this world. Use us God in every way you see fit, every ounce of courage with-in us is at your disposal. Take these ten men and let us grow into ten thousand warriors. Forgive us when you question our actions and lead us when we are in doubt and thank-you for choosing us and giving the honor of living or dying for a cause that has been born within us, that we may stand when others may lose their courage that we may move forward when others may run, that will speak out while others hold their voices in fear of self preservation. Thank-you for this task and may we never let you down, amen."

"Amen," came from the nine others.

Six of the men piled into the small six passengers SUV and began their track back home, leaving the Bishop, Ben, Jordan and Jason waiting for transportation that the Bishop had arranged. After about and hour of updating each other about what they could remember about their adventures involving Oz, Jason asked the Bishop if he knew of anyone that would benefit by killing us." The Bishop paused as if thinking the question through with out a hunch. He appeared to be in pain when he finally answered.

"Yes I do, I feel absolutely sure that the man that spearheaded the attack against us was a local cardinal named Scottman. He is a known child abuser within the ranks of the church. He has very strong ties at the Vatican and a persuasive agreement pertaining to the sexual rights of a priest. I know that he is very high on the totem pole through out this area and maybe the upper east coast.

"He is one that all molestation is reported to and he's the one that shuffles priest from one area to another when they are caught with their hand in a cookie jar. His way of retribution is to give them access to another parish. I am almost sure that he is the one that would suffer most if the recently missing five young boys were discovered. I understand that they were molested again and again over the last couple years with his knowledge. I hope that they haven't been disposed of permanently by these snakes and they've found someway to keep them from our ability to realize their where-about."

"Do you know where he might be now?" asked Jason.

"Oh yes, there's no doubt that he lives lavishly in his well protected luxury home; probably with some willing and unknowing young boy. By now he has probably been told that his plan to destroy all of us at once has worked," answered the Bishop.

"Are you thinking what I'm thinking?" asked Ben while raising one of his eyebrows.

"I think I am. I would like a shot at him while I'm a fully conscience man."

"Yes, so would I, but getting anywhere near him is as hard as getting to the pope himself," said the Bishops. "I think I might have a way to lure him out. After a snowstorm like this he has got to answer the distress calls from his Parishioners. Let's give him a call from a mother with a young boy. I don't think he will be able to resist the temptation. And if we can get our hands on him he may lead us to the missing boys. I personally believe they are still alive.

Jason responded by saying "Let's get his ass and feed him to the public."

"You know what I'd like to do to him. But of course that would be a capital crime," said Ben.

"You know this may work. Especially since he thinks he has eliminated his god sent enemies. He had to know one of us would eventually get to him and punish him without mercy. This may be better, if we can get to him as men. I believe he is totally aware of us in our angelic state. My guess is that that's how he was able to in trap all of us as humans. Here's a plan," said Jason. "First of all, do you have a phone number that he will answer?"

"Yes, I think so. During times of catastrophe all the Bishops can call on their cardinals for advice on spiritual matters. We may not talk to him directly but he will pass on the message right away. Of that, I am sure."

"Okay, here's my next question. How well do you know the layout of his Holy fortress?"

"I know where he sleeps and I know that once he closes his bedroom doors no one will disturb him."

"Do you think the young boys could be held some where in the Perish?"

"Yes, but again, he is powerful and all that work under him is as loyal and as self sacrificial priest can be."

"Yes but, do you think he will open his bedroom doors if he has been tempted with easy access to an eight-year-old boy that he believes to be willing?"

"Of course," answered the Bishop "He can't help himself. I believe they would relieve him as cardinal if he didn't have so much scandalous information about the Catholic hierarchy in Rome. But there is another concern. He has protected himself by employing professional armed guards. I believe there are four of them on duty at all times."

"That may be a problem but I think I have a solution. How many others are on the complex?"

"There are about thirty or so Nuns but they are living in the west wing where they are being trained. They are seldom seen after dark. There are priest that are housed in the South wing but like Nuns they are seldom seen. The security office is in the center of what is considered the lobby. The Cardinal's living quarters are located in the north wing. It has at least four entry doors and a series of alarms to protect the art works and valuables of the church. The artifacts are on the first floor and the cardinals are located on the top second floor."

"Is there a rear entry door to the second floor quarters of the cardinal?"

"Yes it is said that it is used to bring his young subjects to him without drawing attention," said the Bishop. "A good thing is that the security is essentially there to protect the valuable artwork and historic writings. I don't think the cardinal has ever been concerned for his safety."

"Well as of now he should be. The question is what we will do with him when we get him. How do we turn him over to the authorities? If the boys are not there we'll have no proof other than our premonitions and they won't go far against a cardinal that has served the poor and that has helped those in need of prayers for more than twenty years."

"Yeah, and don't forget that he has helped himself and others to hundreds of young boys during that twenty years," said Jordan

"Yes he has and that's why we are here to risk our lives," said Ben.

"What do you think Bishop?" asked Jason.

"I think that if they're not there, then they are dead," Jason said and asked if the Bishop knew of an address North of Chicago towards Milwaukee that they could use as a destination for his plan.

"I do," spoke Jordan. "I have a very close friend that lives twenty minutes south of Milwaukee and he will do anything I ask. The address is 2321 Route 21 south."

"Good," said Jason "That will work perfectly. Once we're on the road back to Chicago I need you to head there and call me when you are close enough to help set our trap." Just then a Humvee pulled up to the front of the Parish and the driver blew the horn. It was still mid-morning but Jason wanted to step up the plan. "We'll talk more when we're in the vehicle."

"Let's get the hell out of here and catch our rat. Or is it a snake? Whatever. Let's just get his ass," said Ben.

On the way back to Chicago Jason began to reveal his plan. He called Helen in Pittsburgh and gave her the cardinal's direct number. He told her that when he called her back he wanted her to call and tell him that she was of the Bishops Perish and she caught her eight-year-old and her nine-year-old being sexually intimate. When she questioned them they informed her that their stepfather, her current husband taught them what to do. Against their will she had him arrested but they promised her that they would never stop. She was to say that she would like to give custody over to the church to teach them the ways of Christ so they could grow up to be normal boys. She had to lock them in their room because they immediately attempted to run away even though the weather was terrible. Please, she was to say, send someone to get them today of they may become dangerous to themselves. They are both handsome young boys with blonde hair and blue eyes but all they think about is sex. Say, please come and get them now! And give them the address I'm about to give you. And honey … make sure it sounds real. It is a matter of life or death, maybe even mine. Jason hung up after a few more encouraging words about his own safety. .

"I think he will send a couple of his security men to get his gift. We'll have Jordan waiting to give them a welcome. Do you think you can handle them?"

"Are you kidding?" was Jordan's response. He was 6' 5" and weighed about 300 lbs. with no fat. "With pleasure," he said.

Jason ask the Bishop if he could put his hands on a robe on something that would fool the cardinal into opening the rear door to accept his two gifts.

"Yes," was the answers. "What do you want to do?" The Bishop asked.

"Just be ready near that back door in case something goes wrong. Can you get a weapon?"

"Yes but I won't, I'm not about to shoot anyone, well at least not while I'm awake."

"Yeah, well go to sleep while you're waiting so we can do this right," said Ben.

"More importantly," said Jason. "I'd like you to be ready in case there are children some where in his living quarters that need to be freed. If there are you call the police while Ben and I take the cardinal for a ride. If there are no children then we'll have to turn the cardinal over to you to pursue his transgression however you see fit. Is it a deal?"

"Yes it's a deal," responded the Bishop. "It's going to be one hell of a day. After last nightwhat worst could happen?" asked the Bishop.

"Well … the three of us could end up dead this time … I'm going to give Helen the green light to call the Cardinal. Do you think we need another prayer?" Ben asked the Bishop.

"No I don't. God is doing this himself. There's no other way so much can happen in a single day without God's input. No … I would say he knows, and we are just tools again, only this time we are all awake … I think … are we awake or are we asleep?" he asked Jason.

"I hope we stay awake, I need to do this as a man. Oz has done more than his share and I'm sure he's not done."

"Amen to that," said Ben. "That's my kind of talk. This Stage is set. The next scene will be us standing on his chest with my pistol up his nose and four or five happy families reunited with their sons."

"Now that does deserve an Amen," said Jason.

†

There are as many as 70 million sex offenders
known to the FBI

†

*"I think rapist should be imprisoned in a population of nothing b
ut sex offenders; to serve their sentence under the constant threat
of being violently raped or murdered the minute they
let their guard down"*

— A woman on the street

CHAPTER TEN

The ride took less than an hour and a half. Jordan wasted no time heading up towards Milwaukee and setting up his part of the plan at his friends' home. The Bishop, Jason and Ben used the Humdi to proceed with what was going to be a night of reckoning for either themselves or the cardinal. At 4:45 it had began to get dark. The snow had long stopped falling but the snow drifts coupled with the cold temperatures and Chicago wind made for a night that most people tried to find shelter inside. They pulled up about two hundred feet from the rear gate that was overlooked by the cardinal's bedroom. With the lights off they sat waiting for the security men to receive their instruction of picking up the two boys. Jason's phone rang startling all three men. It was Helen. She said that they had passed her directly through to speak with the cardinal.

"I told him about the boys and where they were. He said he understood the urgency and would send someone to get them. At first he said tomorrow morning but I convinced him that it had to be right now. I will bring them down to the church at 2321 Rte. 21 South. I had enough of their sinful ways and couldn't make it through another night. He finally agreed and said he would have some one pick them up." Within minutes a van head lights popped on and they watched as two men drove by them in a hurry. Step one went as planned, two were gone and a cardinal was now waiting for his prey.

"All right Benjamin do your thing," Jason said to Ben. Ben got out of the Humdi and walked the whole block to the front of the two stories huge complex. He showed his badge to the front gate keeper that happened to be nearly asleep while watching a football game on his small screen portable. Without hesitation he walked pass and stated that he was here to talk to his security friend at the front desk.

"He's expecting me; you just go head and enjoy the game," Ben said as he gave a friendly wave. When he got to the front locked door, he rattled it hard and drew the attention of the guards inside. The two plain clothed men hurried to the door and again used his badge by pressing it against the window and informing the two of them that there had been an accident at the rear exit and two of the security men on their way out were injured and asked him to come and get their help. An ambulance is on the way. They don't appear to be hurt that badly but they need to be checked over. As Ben was speaking the larger of the two security guards had turn off the alarm and opened the door to exit.

"You stay here and watch the cameras on my side. I'll be back after I make sure George is all right."

Ben turned as if in a panic and led the security man back towards the front gate. "No," the security guard said. "This way, follow me there's a passage way to the back gate that takes a shorter route."

As soon as they got out of sight Ben casually told him, while holding his gun to his ribs, "I need you to stop right now and give me your weapon and put your hands behind your back. Don't make me have to shoot you. Just do as I say big guy." The guard hesitated but obviously decided to do what was asked of him. Ben cuffed him to and iron hand rail and tied his own wool scarf over his mouth.

"It's a little cold out here, but I'll make sure your not here long," Ben told the man as he headed back towards the main entry door. Ben walked up to the same door and rattled it again.

"He told me to come back and use the hard line phone at his post to call the cardinal and tell him that he was going to ride in the ambulance and make sure one of his men would be okay. The other man is uninjured and is coming back here to assist you with security!" Ben said in a hurried fashion. The guard opened the door and pointed Ben towards the security post. The guard was asking questions as they walked but Ben just walked faster and babbled words urgently and undistinguishable. When they got behind the secure area Ben pulled his gun again and told the guard to sit down and not to touch anything. Ben rolled a chair to the middle of the room and assisted the guard down into it.

"I'm not going to hurt you sir. This is not about you or any kind of robbery," Ben told the guard as he used a second pair of cuffs to lock him to the chair. Ben got on the Cellphone to Jason to inform him that both guards were under his control. And that he was in the process of remotely unlocking the rear second floor door that led to the Cardinal's quarters. In the mean time Jordan had intercepted the two other guards and had both of them handcuffed in the rear of the van.

Jason and the Bishop headed up the rear steps for the confrontation with the cardinal. Jason got over anxious and urged the Bishop to knock on the door and report the same fictitious accident to the Cardinal.

"Two of the security guards were leaving the complex and had an accident near the rear gate," he shouted when the cardinal asked who was there. The Cardinal unlatched the door and began to open it when he realized that something wasn't right he pushed the door back to the closed position and began putting on the latches as quickly as he could. Jason realized what was happening and rushed his shoulder against the half locked door and busted it open knocking the Cardinal to the floor and Bishop was left standing in the door as Jason forcefully landed himself onto the Cardinal. There was a brief scuffle between the two men before the Bishop joined in and subdued the Cardinal.

"What's this all about!" ask the Cardinal.

"Just hold still and I'll tell you," said Jason. The Cardinal looked at the Bishop and repeated his question calling the Bishop by name.

"Get off of me," demanded the Cardinal. Before either Jason or the Bishop could respond the Cardinal reared up and threw both men off of him with ease.

He jumped to his feet and turned to face Jason.

"I know you, your Oz. I thought your ass was dead. And you … you sorry excuse for a hero," he said while looking directly at the Bishop.

"This time I'll do the job myself." As he moved forward Ben grabbed him from behind with his forearm around the front of his neck.

"Oh I should have known Ehsa would be here too," he said, as he attempted to maneuver Ben over his shoulder. Buy now Jason was back upon his feet and had locked his arm around the Cardinal's right arm taking away some of his leverage against Ben. All three men went to the floor. But the cardinal managed to get up first. Right away the Bishop was upon his back as Ben was getting to his feet. Ben looked into the eyes of the Cardinal. They were pitch black and wide open. His voice was booming and raspy as he easily tossed the Bishop to the floor and awaited Ben again.

"This is a joke. You three wan'na be heroes, trying to subdue me. All three of you will die and I'll throw you into the vault with the little sex toys that your trying to save," he said.

Jason had hit the floor and was apparently knocked out cold; just cold enough to some how bring on the bright orange eyes of Oz. While awakening Oz stood up and screamed,

"Wait! This fight is now between you and me!"

"Oh I see now, I forgot that none of you has the ability to bring on the strength given to you, now I see," he repeated. "I need to break your neck first and then dispose of the other mini heroes."

Ben had gotten to his feet and attempted one of his strong holds on the cardinal from behind only to be knocked to the floor again.

"They're no match for me and neither are you. After I put you back to sleep I just may f**k all three of you before I put you to sleep permanently."

Ben finally pulled out his weapon without getting up to his feet, but by now both the Cardinal and Oz were struggling to subdue one another and there was no safe shot to take without the chance of hitting Oz.

"Go head, shoot you fool. I'll make sure your bullet enters his head." The Cardinal seemed to be able to keep Oz between himself and Ben's gun. He maneuvered close enough to kick Ben in the head knocking him out cold within seconds. After a few seconds of unconsciousness Ehsa sprung to his feet leaving the gun on the floor. He roared like a beast being set free. The Cardinal managed to throw Oz to the floor and focus on Ehsa with an evil smile. After being thrown to the floor Jason was aroused back to consciousness with Ben's 9-mil gun lying near his head. Jason grabbed the gun while the grinning Cardinal and Ehsa were still facing off. Jason aimed the weapon at the Cardinal and fired three times hoping that bullets would do harm to him. The cardinal looked surprised as his eyes went from totally black to brown with the whites of his eyes back in place. His devious smile changed to fear as he tumbled straight on top of Jason. There was an instant calm and nearly five minutes of silence, until Jason began pushing the body of the Cardinal off of him. . The Bishop and Ben sat quietly as Jason stood up and calmly said, "now what? Some how we've come through the last couple of days in an exhilarated frame of mind that has lead to us three men and a dead Cardinal. What's the reasoning? Where is the reward?"

"Listen," said the Bishop. "Did either of you hear that? It sounded like a computer just activated 'You've got mail.'" This they all heard 'You've got mail' meant that the Cardinal had just received an email and that his computer was turned on. All three men got to their feet and began to look for the source.

"Here it is," said Ben "It's tucked nicely away in the top drawer of his bed stand. It's wide open and ready for a response." Ben set it down on top of the night stand it read 'You have 10 new messages.' Jason hit the 'Read your Messages' with the pointer and up flashed a message from a Cardinal from Spain asking "Did you dispose of the spoiled meat?" It didn't take long for the suspicious minds of the three men to figure out its meaning.

"Look and see what the other messages said," said Ben. A couple Taps on the keyboard by Jason brought up a previous message by the same Cardinal; it said "Get rid of all the videos that contain images of the boys. I have already done so and so have the others. It's time for some new scenery anyway."

"Let's open up some of these video images and see what he's talking about." As Jason hit the buttons the screen adjusted to the still undeleted videos of all four of the boys being sexually abused at different times by different men. Ben happened to glance up at the T.V and monitor what was hung high above the foot of the bed while Jason and the Bishop prowled through the messages of the computer screen. He found the remote control on a shelf above the headboard and clicked it on.

"I think I've found something Jason."

The image of four young boys popped up on the screen. They were filmed lying in a small room, which looked like a padded holding cell. Two of them were curled up in blankets and appeared to be sleep. Their bodies must be some where in this complex. Ben turned up the volume and it drew the attention of the Bishop. When one of the boys cried out;

"I hate this place. I want to go home."

"Those dirty bastards kept those boys in captivity, for heaven knows how long. I'm glad you shot the piece of shit. This is the proof we need to justify our intrusion. And not only that it's my gun and I'm police officer; we'll say that I pulled the trigger and avoid any hardships for Jason. Now all we need to do is find the bodies. Your right their bodies must be some where on this complex."

"Wait!" said Jason. "That's not a video that's a monitor. We're watching them live. They're alive!"

"He's right," said the Bishop. "They are somewhere alive. Thank you, Jesus. My God men let's find them. I'll call 911 to alert the police and bring them into this. In the mean time let's tear this place apart. Here Ben you had better talk to them and who ever is in charge at the police department while me and Jason look around for them."

It wasn't long before the Bishop discovered a rear stairwell that he followed down behind the first floor to a basement level and a room with a vaulted door.

"Here it is!" he shouted "I've found what I think is the rooms entry way."

By now the police had been called by Ben and all three men where standing in front of the door that they hoped the children were behind and alive.

"The lever that opens it is right here to the side but it's locked with a keyed bolt lock," said the Bishop.

"Move," said Ben. Before the Bishop could take two steps Ben fired three times into the bolt lock and watched as it dropped to the floor.

"So much for the lock," Jason said as he and Ben lifted the metal bar that crossed in front of the door. When they pushed the door in the six small boys had gathered tightly together in the rear corner of the room.

"Don't be afraid we've come to take you home. You're safe now," said Jason. The Bishop walked up to them with his hands held out. They drew away in fear and ran around him to Jason's arms.

"It's okay this Bishop is a good man he won't harm you," said Jason.

"Let's get them out of this hell-hole," said Ben. "I need to call the local precinct and tell them to bring someone from social service and the media to witness what has happened here."

The boys were gathered around Jason as he led them up to the first floor and pushed his way into the huge art room which was well lit and probably signaling that the room had been violated by intruders. Jason gathered them together and sat them on a couch that was there for visitors. He kneeled before them and again assured the frightened boys that they were now safe. One of the lads spoke out. "We knew you were coming to take us home. We knew God wouldn't allow them to harm us forever, He told us to hold on, and good men are coming."

"Yeah," said another lad, "We knew … thank you."

"Well it looks like we are all going to make a lot of mothers happy on this day," said the Bishop.

"And a lot of people are going to jail," Ben responded to the Bishop. He also whispered to Jason, "I wish we could have sent a lot more of them with the cardinal."

"Yeah, I do too; but let's let Oz, Ehsa and the rest of the ten do that part. Maybe there will come a day that we can control our counter parts while we are awake. It would be like looking into a mirror and permitting our reflections to use their strength and do what they've been chosen to do. That would be an eye opener for all of the child molesters of the world … So far this has been a ride of a life time for any man. Let's go home Mr. Benjamin."

QUESTIONS AND ANSWERS FROM WOMEN AT LARGE

Questions asked at large to over fifty mothers: All readers are welcome to answer and comment by E-mailing the author at reynoldsjackt@Aol.com

1. What do you think should happen to pedophiles that rape and sometimes kill children under the age of twelve?

2. Would you believe your child if he or she claimed that some one that you love has violated them in a sexual way?

3. Once exposed what if a child molester inside of your well loved family circle tells you that he has confessed to God of his wayward sexual discretions and swears that he will never do it again. Do you except and forgive or do you turn him in to the proper authorities?

4. Describe what you think is the common appearance and mannerism of a pedophile.

5. How should we stop the growing number of sex crimes against small children?

Best answer for number one:

"I think rapist should be imprisoned in a population of nothing but sex offenders; to serve their sentence under the constant threat of being violently raped or murdered the minute they let their guard down"

Most common answer:

"I think they should cut off his penis and throw him in prison forever."

Best answer for number two:

"Without a doubt; I would call the authorities and have my child examined and, that someone that I thought was worth loving; I'd make sure he is judged and thrown into prison; that is if I can resist trying to kill him myself."

Most common answer:

"Yes, but I'd have to be sure that it happened."

Best answer for number three:

"They all say they'll never do it again once they are caught. God may forgive them upon death but my understanding is that most of them will do it again and again every opportunity that they get. Their uncontrolled lust is much stronger than their compassion for whose life they may have destroyed."

Answer:

"The Bible says we should forgive and let God be the judge. Some times prayer can work wonders and we have all sinned at one time or another. Once a man finds Jesus he can change." (Statistics say that he won't change.)

Best answer of number four:

"Gee, I don't know, I've heard that they come in all shapes and colors from twelve years old to ninety. And I think their best ally is deception; kind of like the serpent in the bible."

In proximity of a common answer:

"Some dirty old white man that's made his way into the neighborhood selling candy and ice cream."

Best answer of number five:

"We've got to let young mothers know that we can not leave our babies in any situation where there may be a possibility of harm. Suspect everyone; it's better safe than sorry. We should always be aware of anything or anyone that seems suspicious or unusual when comes to some man trying to be alone with our children for what ever the reason. Our babies depend on us to love and keep them safe, I think we should be mothers twenty four seven."

Common answer:

"We've got to keep our children away from perverts. And the system has got to start giving molesters longer jail sentences."

COMMENTS FROM WOMEN WHO HAVE EXPERIENCED RAPE:

"Most of the individuals that you asked were men except for the woman on the street. I think the person should be beat physically until they are bent over in pain so the only thing on their mind is how much pain they are in and wouldn't be able to think of sex. Every time they think of sex they would be beat again and again until they have no desire for sex with a child, teenage or adult ever again. Because thinking of doing the act is the same as doing it so as long as they can remember the pain of being beat hopefully that will beat the sex urge right out of them. Me being a teenage rape victim forty years ago; I can't forget it nor understand why it was done to me or anyone for that matter. Reading these passages still cause tears and so much pain in my heart for all victims of such a physical and mental violation, which becomes a horrible memory nothing can remove or replace. You can only hope that the effects can be suppressed enough for you to move on and live your life to best of your ability, forgetting is not an option because you never forget. Forgiving, I can say that if I saw that person again I would not forgive them, so I leave that up to God to make that decision on their judgment day. As for me on my judgment day ask me then because at this time I can't forgive someone who made the choice to do these things."

— Mary C. Gaines

†

"How can our legal system adequately dole out retributive justice to the lecherous characters who so easily, so readily, and so thoroughly destroy the most important and precious aspects of being a child. The time in life that we are inherently given to enjoy the simplicity of just living; free of cares or problems, full of trust and love, and totally secure in knowing that nothing or no one can get past Mommy and Daddy to even think about harming you. Then in one fell swoop some morally bankrupt jackass takes that carefree, trusting, secure existence and flushes it. How does an already inadequate legal system even begin to right that wrong. The changes that such a violation creates are devastating and life long. One can only hope that there is some accuracy to the philosophy that 'The energy we send out into the Universe will be returned to us'. I can't imagine any other way of having such an offender adequately punished. In the meantime, being one of those victimized children myself, I keep at my bedside a picture of that little girl at the time in life when she was all the way in it, and I look at the hurt in her eyes and I constantly remind myself to take good care of her. She really needs it."

— H. Bayne

†

What do I think should happen to pedophiles?

This is a hard question for me to answer because I just don't have the capacity of evil in my heart that would match the evil that needs to be destroyed. I think death is too merciful. There are times when I wished for death so that the abuse would end. There was never any mercy for me. I would beg for the abuse to stop but it didn't. I was told I was bad, that I deserved what I got as "punishment". My abuse started with spankings that I got for mouthing off. He told me he wouldn't beat clothes so I had to drop my pants. The spanking morphed into sexual abuse that lasted years and I learned to keep my mouth shut. It didn't matter how much I cried, my feelings were never any concern. Why should the victims every care about how it is effecting the abuser? It was all about him when he was hurting me. The more I cried or begged for him to stop the worst he got. He loved that he could make me beg. He is pure evil and should be destroyed as such. I think torture on daily constant bases would be the only justice. The kind of torture that would have him crying for his mother, begging to die so that it would end. I like the idea of harvesting organs like they do in China. If I would ever see him face to face again I could not be held responsible for my actions. And I do believe I deserve that chance to inflict some of the pain that he caused me. He took away my childhood, my innocents, and my trust in mankind. My husband has never been exposed to abuse or pedophilia and he is much more trusting of the world. He is ok with letting our children play outside which is something that I am envious of. I required constant supervision of my children or I will have panic attacks. I don't believe in the goodness of men anymore. And I don't want to hear any excuses for why they did it. I really don't care. The standard answer is that they were molested as kids; so that gives you the right to someone else? That is bullshit. If you were hurt you would want to do everything you can so that another child would not have to be hurt. All the excuses about "the devil made me do it" is full of crap also, if you have been possessed by the devil than you are evil and must be destroyed. If you are that crazy, if you are that sick, then you need to go. The world is bad enough without people like that.

Would I believe my child if he or she claimed that some one that you love has violated them in a sexual way?

Of course, even if the child just says that they were uncomfortable with someone. That is enough to never let my child around them without supervision. If my child doesn't want to be around someone or left alone with someone I would take that as a cue that something is wrong. That is the first clue. You shouldn't force a child to be with someone they don't like. Most children like everyone, there is a reason if they don't. It is our job as parents to protect our children with our lives if necessary. I don't care who the adult is.

If a child molester was inside of my well loved family circle tells me that he has confessed to God of his wayward sexual discretions and swears that he will never do it again. Would I except and forgive or do I turn him into the proper authorities?

If that person, family member or not, was such a God fearing person they would have never touched a child in the first place. They would be turned into the authorities immediately to be punished for their crime. They can ask for forgiveness from a jail cell.

I can't describe the common appearance or mannerism of a pedophile.

A pedophile could be anyone. Trust no one with your children, ever. There are too many stories out there about people who were the pillars of society who you would never think could do something like that. If a pedophile was scary or ugly they couldn't get a child to trust them to get close enough to scare them into doing what they want without telling.

How should we stop the growing number of sex crimes against children?

By talking about it … My only regret about what happened to me was that I didn't make sure that he was not allowed to hurt someone else. I wanted to go to trial and make him tell everyone what he did. He should have been hunted by the general population so that he could never go near a child again. We also need to tell our children to never keep a secret. That there will always be someone to protect them if there is a problem. There should always be someone they can tell. And that they are not bad and never could be; that they will always be safe at home. Children need to be told in no uncertain terms what inappropriate touching is. That no one should ever touch them or make them touch their private parts. There also needs to be better and more visible punishments for offenders. Everyone should know what a pedophile has done. Most people like to keep quiet about it for the sake of the child. But the child didn't do anything wrong and would probably feel better if they knew that the abuser is being punished. The pedophiles picture and story should be all over the news. They should not be able to get a job or buy a house or go to public places."

— A.E.R.

†

INTERNET DIALOGUE BETWEEN THE AUTHOR AND THE MOTHER OF THREE SEXUALLY MOLESTED CHILDREN

†

To: Jack T Reynolds <reynoldsjackt@aol.com>
Sent: Sat, Feb 26, 2011 3:10 am
Subject: How I felt

I wanted to take the time and write down how I felt when I found out that my two daughters and my son were molested at ages five seven and eight. The monster that molested them took away from them something that they could never get back and that was there virginity. His sin penetrated there souls and It was like having a hammer chisel away at my heart. It almost destroyed me. For years I blamed myself: because I work nights and I left him in my home allowing him to have free reign over them. I will never have complete peace, until he gets what he deserves.

It grieves me to know that she died without having a chance to see him come to justice.

There is also a personal history behind the pain, when I was very young my sister and I were both molested. Our bedroom was upstairs right next to my oldest brother's room and my mom and dad's bedroom was downstairs. So this gave my brother free reign to do what ever he wanted to do to us. All of it was touching but it was still violation of our innocence, but we were afraid to say anything. I believe this is why I married early; it was away to get out of this house and away from what was hurting me. There is no healing of the heart when something like this happens to you or your children.

While my father was trying to protect us, he was unaware that he had a molested right in his own home. My dad would never let us go anywhere he would never let us spend the night at anyone house or sit on any mans lap, but he never told us why and at such a young age we did not know why.

When my son and I talk about what happened to him and his sisters, I can still see the pain in his eyes and feel the hurt. My daughter is a stronger person and very protected over her children even though they are boys. I don't have words to say to her that will heal her hurt. Time will sooner or later erase some of the pain.

For years I was self destructive I did not care about my life nothing ever went well for me and I felt like there was no end to the suffering. I was wrong.

I may feel like writing more I am tired now. I hope this helps."

—JS

†

To: <u>joyls@.com</u>
Date: Sunday, February 27, 2011, 10:39 P.M.

"I had to change a little please see if you approve of the paraphrased quote"

†

To: Reynoldsjackt <reynoldsjackt@aol.com>
Sent: Wed, Mar 2, 2011 9:21 am
Subject: Re: How I felt

I do want to change the fact that my oldest daughter was not the only one that was molested. I want it to read my two daughters and my son was molested. My son was only five at the time. Thanks

†

To: joyls@.com
Date: Wednesday, March 9, 2011, 8:47 AM

Joyce; as I said before, I would like very much if you could tell your own story. Basically about your own fear and the helplessness you must have felt while this was going on. Most people have never experienced true fear and they don't know how powerful it can be. They all reflect what they would have done differently. Being institutionalized at twelve I know what fear can do and I know that it can lead you to a feeling where you believe that only God can help or that it's all your fault and He won't. I would like to expose Mr. Ore's approach and his way of getting away with it in your own perspective. Please give it a try. It will be a way for you to stop his and others like him from walking through life as if they've done nothing wrong and blaming it on the child or the mother. I have delayed going to publishing because I would like to add the inside stories of women that have gone through and survived these so called monsters."

Jackie

†

March 9, 2011

"Sorry I have been really ill. I had a carbon monoxide leak and two gas leaks in the house and I have been suffering from really bad headaches. When I get home this evening I will e-mail you I am at work right now."

†

From: Joyce <joyls@.com>
To: Reynoldsjackt <reynoldsjackt@aol.com>
Sent: Wed, Mar 9, 2011 11:31 p.m.

Okay I will try to let you know how I felt when this molestation took place, it has been a long time and I do my best to block it out of my mind as much as I can. Every time the abuse comes to mind I wonder why me why my daughter, and why did he get away with it. Why did he steal her innocence?

First of all I blamed myself because I let a complete stranger come into my home. I was suffering from very low self- esteem and I had problems with relationships and loneliness. Anytime someone paid any attention to me it sparked my interest in them.

The abuser was very nice he would come over everyday. He spent time at the parks with the children and he also went to church with us. I did know that he came from a big family I felt comfortable around him and his family.

When I became a nurse I worked the day and the night shift which gave him the opportunity to have free reign. When I came home from work it was like everything was normal. She never showed any signs of being abused and I never saw any. I was clue-less when it came to what he was doing to her. When I did find out I immediately took her to a safe place then I went to the house and called the police. I found out later that he had threatened her, by telling her that if she told he would kill me and her and set the house on fire. I always talked to her about telling me anything but fear took over. I did not recognize any change in her behavior no signs of withdrawal … I wonder will he ever pay for what he did to us.

Joyce

†

Excellent, I will modify and send you the slight adjustment. And; yes he will pay he has been paying and he is about to pay a lot more. He will suffer as long as I'm breathing; death is too easy of an escape.

Jackie

†

Pedophilia and sexual violence against children and youth is the worst crime imaginable. But from where I sit, as a woman of African descent, the Black community condones violence against children and women. It would be ridiculous for Black people in this country to continue to look to the US government to address the issue of sexual assault and violence against children and youth and women. For those who look to the criminal justice system to address this issue look closer to the fact put forward by their own experts: *In the US, a woman is raped every 6 minutes; a woman is battered every 15 seconds. A child calls Child Line on average once every hour to talk about rape and other types of sexual abuse.* This country doesn't really care about the assaults on Black children, youth and women because they are unwilling to address this issue.

Sexual violence and assault goes beyond race, class and sex. It speaks to our willingness to look the other way, to condone this type of behavior by doing what we do so well — nothing. Most of the work I do involves working with women and young girls and I can state as fact that the overwhelming majority of these women have been sexually abused in their own homes by brothers, uncles, fathers, family friends, momma's boyfriends, etc. Their families know about it but they don't want' to "get in nobody's business." Not only are the women sexually abused but they are blamed for the abuse by their family and community. As young girls, the women are victimized by an adult in their life then they are removed from their homes. Not one "good man" or "good woman" or god-fearing Christian or righteous Muslim has ever spoken up for these women. It's easy to sit back and say what one would do if someone sexually assaulted a loved one. It's much harder to stand up for someone who no one is standing up for. My position is that to allow anyone to harm a child and not intervene, not at least talk about it or question it, this violation is the epitome of self-hatred.

Until we — as a people — stand up for the most vulnerable of our people against sexual assault and violence we are nothing but talk. And talk is something that we as Black people love to do the world over. We talk but we don't do.

— Sabira Bushra,. Community advocate

TEN GOOD MEN:

About Us … In the name of God we have joined together to fulfill a mission of godliness. We will come to the aid of each other and all women and children. We pledge to live up to the title of good and stout hearted men; as one of ten we will multiply to ten thousand and more; never abandoning our objective to be ready and able to step-up and say, 'We are here to extend a helping hand and when ones hands are not enough we will call for ten and when ten is not enough we will call for the hands of ten thousand. We honor one another as good men who will take on the challenge of assuring those who would otherwise suffer greatly, that if there comes a time that someone is in need of our strength, we will stand tall enough to overshadow their desperation …We stand not only shoulder to shoulder but heart to heart in our solemn pledge to aid, protect and carefor those that may not be able to care for themselves.

— Yours Truly, One of Ten

Jack Reynolds

Note:

Some of the proceeds from the sell of this book will be used to assist in ongoing efforts of The Ten Good Men in their pursuit to watch over and protect our children everywhere.

For additional information please contact; Jack Reynolds at Reynoldsjackt@aol.com, C.M. Clayton at thaclaytons@yahoo.com or Ben Ashe at aasheboy@aol.com

As disturbing as some of these stories are they are mild compared to the realities that go on in the lives of children that are captive to anin-home predator.

Wake up! Don't let a child fall victim to pedophilia. Never underestimate the overpowering strength of uncontrolled lust or what it can make a person capable of. Give a predator an opportunity; add an excuse of alcohol, drugs or a mystic devil and you may find someone you love has fallen to the temptation of self indulgence.

A child's monster often lies within his or her own home as an idol minded, selfish man that somehow justifies his actions long before he has to deny his acts after he is discovered.

Please, for the sake of our children; take away the opportunity…

Chapter Quotes by: Dr. C.M. Clayton, Ben Ashe, Charles Reynolds, Doug Huggins, Rocco Reynolds, Ahmad Hakeem, Anthony Jones, Charles Gaines Jordan Reynolds,

ABOUT THE AUTHOR

Jack Thomas Reynolds has written five books

The Ethiopian Woman
While Angels Watched
Up Through the Cracks
Oz One of Ten
Tricked

He was born in a small coalmining town just outside of Pittsburgh Pa. He is the father of six daughters. He has always loved art and the art of telling stories; his own and the stories of others he has come to know.

He himself came up through the cracks at a time when a black man falling through cracks was very easy to achieve. He blames all of his positive achievements on the fact that he has always abstained from mind altering substances; drugs, alcohol and tobacco. He blames his shortcomings on his own stubbornness. If he had a motto it would be that there is nothing on earth stronger than love and comradeship …" Written by a friend

"I was not born to be alone. I will always need someone to tell my stories too. When someone is beside me I am much stronger because they are a blessing to me. When I stand behind someone they can rest assured that they have a faithful comrade. If I should ever lead someone it will never be against God. If I should fail to defend the innocence within children it will not be because I did not do my best, it will be because I died." — Jack Reynolds